MW00469187

TOP TROUBLE

A SUBMISSIVE SERIES STANDALONE NOVEL

TARA SUE ME

Praise for Tara Sue Me

"An erotic, deeply loving BDSM romance...Fans of erotic romance will delight in its mix of heat and heart." **PUBLISHERS WEEKLY starred review for THE MASTER**

"For those Fifty Shades fans pining for a little more spice...the Guardian recommends Tara Sue Me's Submissive Trilogy, starring handsome CEO Nathaniel West, a man on the prowl for a new submissive, and the librarian Abby, who is yearning for something more." **LOS ANGELES TIMES**

"Scorching sex, well-developed characters, occasional bursts of humor, and skillful plotting make Me's series launch a must-read." **PUBLISHER WEEKLY on AMERICAN ASSHOLE**

Copyright © 2019 by Tara Sue Me

All rights reserved.

No part of this book may be reproduced in any form or by any electronic or mechanical means, including information storage and retrieval systems, without written permission from the author, except for the use of brief quotations in a book review.

ISBN ebook: 9781950017096

ISBN Print: 9781950017102

Cover photo: Depositphotos.com

Chain Elements: Pixabay.com

Cover Design: Mister Sue Me

❀ Created with Vellum

Chapter One

Until tonight, Evan Martin had never felt jealous of a submissive. But watching the man across the room kneel at Kelly Bowman's feet and seeing the way she talked to him, her hand in his hair, and her lips brushing the skin along his ear… Well, it had him thinking things he'd never admit to anyone.

He took a step away from the wall he'd been leaning against to shift his feet and calm his dick down.

"Looks like Mistress K has herself a playmate for the evening."

Evan looked up and found Daniel, one of the group's long term Doms, watching the curvy redhead.

"Yeah," Evan said. "He's played with her before. He knows what he's getting into."

Daniel raised an eyebrow.

"Not that I keep track of who she plays with or anything,"

Evan hurried to add, even though he did. She hadn't played with anyone the last two times the group met here at their new club. It had been six months since she played with the sub she was talking to at the moment.

Daniel obviously overlooked his bald-faced lie. "She brings so much to the group, even apart from being our only Senior Domme. She'll be missed."

Evan's head spun back to Daniel so fast he was surprised he didn't give himself whiplash. "What? What do you mean, missed?"

Daniel cringed. "I didn't realize you hadn't heard. She took a job in Texas. With the Dallas PD."

Kelly was moving? To Dallas?

"No," Evan replied, trying to sound as normal as possible. "I hadn't heard that. I wish her all the best." He couldn't imagine her not being in Delaware. Not being part of the group. "When's she moving?"

"A month, I think." Daniel wrinkled his brow. "Julie wants to throw her a party, but she's too busy with wedding stuff."

Daniel and his submissive, Julie, were getting married in three months. Evan nodded but said nothing. He found that he couldn't. Daniel looked at him as if expecting him to be a smartass about Kelly moving, her potential party, or both. But the snark wouldn't come. In its place was something else. Evan couldn't quite put his finger on it, but it felt an awful lot like regret.

He felt a sudden need to get away from Daniel. The senior Dominant was too observant, and he'd known Evan for too long. He'd keep talking about Kelly, and if Evan didn't watch himself, he'd end up confessing his attraction to her.

He wasn't sure why it mattered. So what if he found the Domme attractive? She was every man's fantasy: hot body, fiery red hair, plus she was a hard as nails cop who busted balls for a living. Who wouldn't find her attractive was the real question.

Probably, it was because they were both Tops. A relationship between the two of them would never work. Over the years, it became easier to pick fights with her than to confess he was attracted to her. Not to mention, pushing her buttons was so damn fun.

The sound of giggling caught his attention, and he glanced at the sitting area to his left. A group of unattached submissives had their heads together, whispering about something. He moved toward a vacant chair next to them.

Maybe he'd try to find someone to play with. That would force him to focus on something else. And that would be a good thing, because at the moment, Kelly Bowman filled all the space in his head.

⊙⊙⊙⊙⊙

KELLY WATCHED as the male submissive stood to his feet and walked off. He'd approached her about playing, but she wasn't in the mood. She didn't even know why she'd bothered to show up, other than it was a habit to attend play parties. That should have been a red flag. In what world did she think it was acceptable to show up at a play party just because it was habit? Hell, she should have stayed home. At least then, she could have knocked out some packing.

Now she had to be social. She glanced around the new club, taking in all the friends she'd made over the years.

3

Friends she wouldn't be seeing much of after a month. Though she was a bit apprehensive about moving back to her childhood home state, she was mostly excited.

Her new position was a big promotion. She'd flown to Dallas twice and was looking forward to her new job and getting to know her new colleagues. The housing market was so much more reasonable, and those horrid winters would forever be a thing of her past.

That alone should have her dancing for joy, instead she felt like she was trying to convince herself moving was a good idea.

"Yo, Red. I didn't know you had a cowboy fantasy."

She turned at the sound of Evan Martin's voice and found him leaning against a wall, his dirty blond hair falling haphazardly into his face. In fact, it was so long, only one of his icy blue eyes was visible.

"I'm surprised you could see it was me through that mop on your head you call hair." She pretended to study it. "I hope you didn't drive here. I think your haircut could be an impediment to driving."

His grin grew larger. "If I say yes, will you attempt to handcuff me?"

"You'd like that wouldn't you?"

He pushed back from the wall. "Nah, I'd rather be the one doing the cuffing, and I could tell you why I wear it like this, but it'd be better if I showed you. Of course, one of us would need to be in cuffs and it won't be me."

"You don't have the balls to handcuff me."

"That I do, Red. Would you like to see them?"

"That's okay, I didn't bring my magnifying glass."

"Damn it, you two." Daniel said, coming up beside them. "Mistress K, you're here for another few weeks. Do you think it's possible you and Martin could stay away from each other during that time?"

She rolled her eyes, but the truth was, she enjoyed sparring with Evan. He was funny and sharp and, not to mention, hot as ever-loving hell. On more than one occasion, she'd wondered what it would be like to submit to him. Could she do that? Even though she wasn't a bottom?

He looked at her as if he knew what she was thinking. His eyes danced with barely controlled mirth.

"What's so funny, Martin?" she asked.

"You," he replied. "I know what you're thinking."

"I doubt that." She hoped to hell he didn't know what she was thinking. "You're a lot of things, but brain reader isn't one of them."

"I don't have to be a mind reader to know when a woman wants me."

"If you think—"

"That's enough." Daniel came in-between them now, and he'd lost his jovial expression. "I've warned you both too many times to count. It's time for you to leave. Both of you. You're disruptive and setting a bad example."

Evan looked like he would argue, but Kelly felt nothing but relief. Her rational brain told her she could go home and start sorting through her house, decide what was going with her to Dallas, and what she could either toss or give to charity. But in reality, she knew what would happen, and it involved her favorite vibrator and a fantasy or two starring a smartass Dom. She spun on her heel and headed to the dressing room.

Ten minutes later, she stepped outside only to find Evan standing by her car.

She ignored him and opened her door, when Evan moved closer. "You're welcome in advance for the orgasm."

Chapter Two

Two Weeks Later

"Do you think Kelly's drinking a bit too much?" Evan asked Daniel. He shouldn't care. It was her going away party, after all. If she wanted to get plastered, that was her choice. But...

He looked outside for her car. Yup, her dark sedan was parked outside Daniel's house, which meant she drove herself. She wouldn't be able to drive home, that was a certainty. He should leave his car in Daniel's driveway and take her home. Or would it be better to take his car?

"It does look like she's had quite a few." Daniel frowned. "It's not like her. I don't think I've ever seen her have more than one."

"Maybe the move is getting to her." It sure as hell was getting to him. He'd merely waded through the last two weeks. He didn't want her to leave, but how to convince her to stay?

Why did he continue to think such stupid thoughts? Nothing would keep her in Delaware. If she wanted to move to Dallas, she should move to Dallas. He'd never told her he was attracted to her and now it was too late. Seriously, what did he think would happen? She'd find out he was attracted to her, and she'd cancel her move? Yeah, right.

He should have done or said something years ago. That would have been the smart thing to do. But, no. He'd acted like he had all the time in the world and look where it got him. Standing at a going away party for the one woman he didn't want to go away.

Daniel glanced at his watch. "I'll drive her home. Party's winding down, anyway. Let me go tell Julie."

He started to walk away, but Evan shot his hand out to stop him. "I'll take her home."

Daniel raised an eyebrow. "You will?"

"Yes, if you don't mind, I'll leave my car in your driveway."

"And you'll get her home in one piece?"

"I'm insulted you'd think otherwise."

"I've broken up more spats between the two of you than I can count on both hands and that's just this year alone. You have to admit it sounds peculiar that you'd be the first one volunteering to drive her home."

"I enjoy picking on her, that doesn't mean I want anything bad to happen to her."

Daniel gave him the look he gave people when he knew they weren't being completely honest.

"Okay, fine." He might as well tell someone, and Daniel would understand. "I like her. Is that what you want to hear? I like her, and it's too damn late to do anything about it because she's moving to fucking Dallas. So the least I can do is drive her home after she's had too much to drink at her going away party."

There. He'd said it. Out loud. He waited for the "Ah, ha! I knew it," from Daniel, but it didn't come.

"So sorry, man. I can't imagine how tough that must be." He clapped his hand on Evan's shoulder. "Take her home."

"Thanks." Maybe he should have talked with Daniel about Kelly months, heck, years ago. If he had, would she still be moving? There was no way to know. Besides, what was done was done. He couldn't change anything. With a sigh, he headed toward Kelly and braced himself for what he knew would be an unpleasant argument.

She stood talking with a few of the other women in their group. Sasha and Julie on one side. Abby on the other. For a second, he thought she looked sober, but Abby said something the other ladies laughed at, only Kelly also swayed. Nope. No driving for her.

Sasha stepped aside at his approach. Abby crossed her arms and gave him the evil eye. Clearly, the women all expected him to start something. Not that he could blame them, if this had been a party for any other reason, that's exactly what he'd be doing.

But it wasn't any other party, it was Kelly's going away

party, and he didn't plan on starting anything with Kelly tonight. Not what they thought anyway.

"Mistress K?" he asked, deciding that was the quickest way to get everyone on the same page.

He didn't look to see how the other women reacted, he only watched Kelly. She narrowed her eyes. "Why did you call me that? Did hell freeze over and no one told me?"

He decided both of those were rhetorical questions. "I'll drive you home."

She'd already been planning her cutting comeback in her head, he could tell. But his reply hadn't been the one she'd expected and her mouth snapped shut. He'd expected her to argue with him, but then again, she was a police officer and would know she was in no condition to drive home.

"I should check for flying pigs on the way home," Abby said to Sasha in an *I'm-not-even-trying-to-be-quiet* whisper.

"Okay," Kelly said. "Ready to leave?"

"Yeah," he replied, still stunned by her reaction. "Whenever you are."

She said her goodbyes and hugged the remaining partygoers. More than a few raised an eyebrow at the two of them. Kelly grabbed her purse. "I'm ready."

He nodded and held out his hand. "We'll take your car."

Once she handed him the keys, they were on their way. She lived about twenty miles from Daniel's, and because of the time of night, it didn't take long at all to reach her place. He parked in her driveway, and she only gave him a slight raised eyebrow when he accompanied her to the front door. He passed her the keys.

"Come inside," she said, unlocking the door.

He hesitated.

"Now," she said.

Fuck, but that Domme voice turned him on more than he'd let anyone know. Especially her.

"Only because you asked so politely," he said, breezing past her and entering the house.

"There he is. I knew he was in there somewhere."

"What are you talking about?"

"Asshole Evan."

He bit his tongue to keep from replying and looked around the house. His chest hurt when he noticed the cardboard boxes stacked everywhere. Like he needed a reminder she was moving. She'd hosted the Partner group over the years, before they had built the new club building, so he was familiar with her house. He couldn't help but think it looked so clinical without the tiny evidences of her touch.

But some small part of him rejoiced that there hadn't been a FOR SALE sign in her yard.

"When are you going to list?" he asked.

"Sometime the next week, I think." She made her way toward the kitchen. "I'm going to get some water. You want some?"

He sat down. "No. I'm good."

She returned minutes later, glass in hand. He should go, it hurt too much to stay in the room with Kelly and her packed up boxes. The entire house seemed to mock him. *Yeah, you're finally here*, it said. *Three years too late.*

He made a move toward the door, but Kelly nodded to the couch. "Sit."

He told himself he only sat down because he didn't want to leave, anyway. It had nothing to do with following Kelly's orders. But he'd be lying if he didn't admit that Kelly giving commands was hot.

She sat down beside him and gave him the once over. Evan leaned back into the couch and tried to act as if they did this every day. "Like what you see?"

Her answer was to run a manicured nail down his thigh. "You work out."

He gave a grunt in reply. Partially because she hadn't posed it like a question and partially because hot damn, he liked it when she touched him.

"I bet you look great with your shirt off," she said in a low and throaty voice that had him harder than hell.

He closed his eyes as her hand inched its way upward and teased the hem of his shirt. God, but he wanted to yank the damn thing off and let her have her fill of him. But she was drunk and if she wasn't, she was too tipsy to give consent.

Figures, the one time he was able to do something with Kelly, he wouldn't allow himself to. It had to be some sort of cosmic payback for all the grief he'd given her over the last few years.

Her hand slipped under his shirt and stroked his stomach. Fuck, what her touch did to him.

"Tell me you want me, Evan." Her nails scratched him, and he gripped the arm of her couch so hard, he feared he caused permanent damage to the material.

"You're drunk," he managed to ground out. Perhaps if he said it out loud, it'd keep him from doing something stupid.

"I'm not that drunk."

"You are and you'll regret this in the morning." She attempted to slip her fingers under his waistband. He attempted to stand. "I should go."

She pulled him back down. "Sit."

"Kelly." Damn it all to hell, if she kept this up, there was no way he'd be able to resist her.

"I'm going to tell you a secret." She brushed his upper thigh, and he gritted his teeth. She no longer attempted to get her hands under his pants, but her touch over his pants was just as distracting.

"I don't know if now's the best time to be spilling secrets." He should get some sort of award for the self-control he was showing. "Don't say anything you'll regret."

"I don't fuck the men I Top."

Wait. What?

He slapped his hand down on top of hers. He needed to think clearly and that wouldn't happen with her wandering fingers. "Say that again."

"I don't fuck the men I Top."

Jesus. Why was she telling him this? "Kelly, I…" he started but didn't know what to say.

"It's been so long." She freed her hand and cupped his erection. "I don't want to move to Dallas. Give me a reason to stay."

"Kelly." He shifted on the couch, so he could look into her eyes. "I can't-"

She stopped him from saying anything else by pressing her lips to his. One touch of her mouth and all his carefully constructed arguments flew out the window. Hell, he wasn't a saint by anyone's definition and her lips... Hot damn, her lips were sweeter than anything he'd ever imagined.

He moved closer to her, cupping her head in his hands, and titling his head so he could deepen the kiss. She parted her lips with a whimper, and he was gone. She pushed his shirt up, and he pulled back to jerk it off.

"Look at you," Kelly said, running her hands up and down his abs.

Her touch was heaven, and he'd never been happier that he worked out. All those early morning jogs and push ups were well worth it for the look of appreciation in Kelly's eyes. She dropped her head to kiss his chest, and he bit back a moan.

He slipped his hands into her long, red hair and it was just as soft and silky as he'd imagined. At the moment, he had a vision of her riding him, all that hair dancing around her shoulders as he thrust up into her. He tightened his grip on the soft strands.

Another image flashed in his mind: Kelly on her knees, his cock in her mouth and those gorgeous red waves brushing his thigh as she took him deeper and deeper. Later. Maybe not tonight, but soon.

Her hands fumbled with his zipper and she cursed softly when she found herself unable to pull the tab down. He reached a hand down to help, but when she sat up, he looked in her eyes. Damn it all to hell, what was he doing?

Her eyes had a hazy look, which told him all he needed to know. She was still under the influence of the alcohol she'd had at the party. He couldn't continue.

It was the hardest thing he'd ever done, but he pulled back and shifted away from her. "We can't tonight, Kelly. Not like this."

"Not like what?"

"You're drunk. I won't take advantage of you."

She reached for him again, but he shook his head.

"It's not taking advantage of me if I'm the one asking for it," she said.

"All the more reason for me to stop this before it goes any further."

"You don't want me?"

Hell, she wasn't going to get all weepy now, was she? "I didn't say that. I said not right now. Later. When you're sober."

She looked uncertain for the first time. No matter how drunk she was, she recognized rejection when she heard it. And he hated that because he didn't want to say no. He didn't want to turn her down. He wanted to pick her up and carry her to bed and keep her occupied until there was no way she'd even think about moving to Dallas.

And then, just because he'd like it, he'd keep her there for a little while longer.

"Kelly." He stroked her cheek. "Trust me when I tell you that there is nothing I want more than to continue this. But I've waited for you too damn long to do something you won't remember or might regret in the morning."

He kept his gaze on hers, trying to convince her with all that he had in him that he was telling the truth. He wasn't sure she got his message, though. She nodded and rose to her feet. "Okay. I'll just go on to bed."

She got up and walked down the hallway, disappearing into her bedroom. For a few seconds, he just sat there. Now what was he supposed to do? She was just going to leave him alone? She must be drunker than he thought.

He stood up and waited for her to come back. Surely, she was coming back. But when five minutes passed and she didn't reappear, he walked down the hall toward her bedroom. The door was open, so he stuck his head in.

"Kelly?"

A snore came from the bed.

"Damn," he muttered under his breath. She had undressed down to her underwear, but didn't make it under the covers. He hesitated for a minute before taking the light blanket at the foot of the bed and pulling it over her.

He couldn't leave now, there was no way to lock her door. With a heavy sigh he walked back into the living room. Looked like it was the sofa for him tonight.

Chapter Three

Kelly opened her eyes and immediately regretted the decision to do so. With a groan, she closed them, throwing a pillow over her head for good measure. What the hell had gotten into her last night? She couldn't remember the last time she got drunk, but it was probably back in her college days.

She hoped to God she hadn't done anything stupid, but unfortunately, she couldn't remember much of the evening. Damn, what did she remember? It hurt her head, but she tried to think back.

Daniel and Julie had hosted the party at their house, which was crazy because they were getting married in less than three months. However, they both refused for anyone else to host. Daniel had said it was for "old time's sake."

But whatever.

Kelly recalled being tipsy and laughing with Sasha over something Abby said. Dena had been there earlier but she was in her third trimester and her husband, Jeff, had called their evening short. Evan came by while she was chatting with Sasha and Abby.

Evan?

Footsteps sounded coming down her hallway.

She sat up, reaching for her service weapon out of instinct, but it wasn't on her nightstand where she normally kept it. Damn it, did she have anything she could use for a weapon? She spied her purse on the floor. No doubt her phone was in there and more than likely, dead.

"Kelly?" Her door creaked open.

"Evan?" she asked, and a flood of memories came rushing back. Evan driving her home and her asking him to come inside. Sitting on the couch with him. Talking. Kissing. His shirt coming off.

Her hand flew to her mouth. *They hadn't, had they?*

She didn't think so, seeing as she wasn't naked.

"I didn't wake you up, did I?" he asked. "I didn't mean to if I did; just wanted to check on you. Daniel and Julie will be here in about an hour or so to drop off my car."

Her brain was too jumbled to form words, much less speak them. She nodded to let him know she'd heard then grimaced in pain because nodding hurt.

"I can get you some water and aspirin if you'd like," he said.

For some reason that irritated her. It was her house. What the hell was he doing standing there acting like it was any

18

of his business if she wanted water or aspirin for crying out loud?

She sat up in bed, doing her best to ignore the pounding of her head. "I can get it myself, need to get up any way."

"I was going to make you something for breakfast but I wasn't sure if you'd be hungry when you woke up or if the thought of food would make you feel sick." He stepped aside and averted his eyes as she hurried by him.

"I'm not in the mood for anything right now." She snatched the closest clean items she could find and hugged them to her chest. "You can fix yourself something to eat."

Without waiting for him to respond, she stepped into the bathroom and closed the door behind her. She dropped her clothes on the countertop and braced herself to look in the mirror.

Thankfully, she felt worse than she looked. Since she'd been in college the last time she had a hangover this bad, she couldn't remember how it impacted her appearance. Not that she cared how she looked to Evan.

Maybe if she kept telling herself that, she'd eventually believe it.

She splashed cold water on her face and pulled her hair back into a ponytail. A longer than normal toothbrushing rounded out all she felt like doing at the moment. It was just her luck she happened to pick up a pink t-shirt. Evan had forever teased her about wearing pink. She didn't care if redheads weren't supposed to wear the color, she liked it and therefore she'd wear it.

Holding her head high, she walked out of the bathroom and down the hall to her kitchen and Evan.

He stood at her stove, cooking something, and turned to give her his mischievous grin.

"You really are cooking breakfast," she said because it didn't fit the image she had of him at all.

"Just pancakes." He shrugged. "I thought they'd be bland enough that if your stomach was off, you might be able to at least eat a few bites."

Cooking Evan shocked her. Cooking and thoughtful Evan sent her mind in a whirlwind. Though she might be tempted to chalk the whirlwind up to her hangover, that wouldn't be the entire truth.

She'd been attracted to him when all he ever showed her was his sarcastic side. Now that she had proof he could be thoughtful and caring? Hell, why was she only finding this out now that she was leaving?

"Can I help?" she asked.

"I'm almost finished," he said. "But if you don't mind grabbing a few plates, I'll get these on the table."

Five minutes later, they were sitting at her table eating a breakfast she'd never in a million and two years imagined ever taking place. And the fact that Evan's pancakes were some of the best she'd ever had? Icing on the cake.

"So why Dallas?" he asked, lifting his fork up to take a bite.

"I grew up there. A lot of my family is still there, and a few friends. You know the kind you can go years without seeing but once you get together it's like you've never been apart?"

"You have friends here." Though he spoke it off-handed,

she couldn't help but wonder if there was more to his statement.

"Yes, and I also have to deal with snow."

He rolled his eyes. "We still get less here than the average person."

"In Dallas, snowfall is basically zero." And she added as if an afterthought. "And it's warmer, too."

"What of your family is in Dallas?"

"My parents and sister are all in Dallas."

"Are your parents still together?"

She smiled at the thought of her parents. "Fifty-seven years and counting."

He whistled. "Wow. That's rare these days."

"Right? And they're not getting any younger. They're both healthy and they still live in the house I grew up in, but all it takes is one fall, a broken hip…" She shook her head, having seen it happen much too often. "I feel as if I should be there."

"Which begs the question, and I have no doubt you'll tell me exactly where to shove it if you want me to shut up, is why did you move to Delaware to begin with?"

Of course that would be his next question. It always was. But usually she could laugh off the reason and somehow she knew she couldn't with Evan. "What reason does any woman leave family and friends behind?"

"Ah." He grinned. "I feel as if I should say a fantastic promotion, but I get the distinct impression that's not why you moved here."

"Sadly, no. I followed a man I thought I was in love with."

He frowned. "When was this?"

"Six years ago, maybe?" If she remembered right, Evan joined the Partners BDSM group five or six months after she did. "He was long gone by the time you joined."

"And after the two of you parted ways, you stayed here instead of going back to Texas?"

"Yes," she said, appreciating the fact he worded it "parted ways" instead of what it really was, being tossed aside like yesterday's garbage. "Part of the reason I stayed was because I'd just got settled in with the Partner's group."

Evan probably assumed her ex had been a submissive since she was a Domme, but that couldn't be farther than the truth. In fact, until her ex left her, she'd only experienced being a submissive. It wasn't until she joined the Partner's group she discovered she was actually a switch.

Though relieved to find she felt at home on either side of the paddle, she also felt alone and somewhat isolated, even among the group's members. Not feeling totally accepted by either the submissives or the Dominants in the group, she'd classified herself as a Domme. Of course, that had been years ago and very few of those who knew her from her early days as a switch were still active members. She doubted they even remembered.

Either way, she wasn't going to share any of that with Evan.

Wanting to change the subject, she asked him, "How did you learn to make awesome pancakes?"

His knowing grin told her he knew she'd only asked him

out of a desperate attempt to avoid further questions about her past. Thankfully he didn't seem to want to call her on it. "Years of practice at pancake breakfast fundraisers."

She remembered he taught high school if for no other reason than it seemed like the very last thing he'd do. "What do you teach again?" She wasn't sure she'd ever heard, especially since she'd never had an actual conversation with him before today.

"American History. Regular. Honors. Advanced Placement."

"No shit?" she asked before she could stop herself, because there was no way she'd heard that before. No way would she have forgotten he taught history.

He laughed at her reply. "For real. No shit."

"I'm sorry. I meant nothing by saying that. Only when I heard you taught, I assumed PE or something like that."

"Nah, I've never been that athletic."

She cocked an eyebrow at him. "I find that hard to believe."

He held up his hand as if taking an oath. "Honest-to-God truth. I suck at all sports."

"Mmm." Kelly still found that hard to believe.

"Let me guess," he said in a teasing voice. "You were a star athlete in high school?"

"Varsity track and field, and girl's varsity basketball team captain."

"I totally called it. Now, tell me why you decided to be a cop."

She wasn't sure she wanted to tell him the whole story, but he'd been honest with her about how horrible he was at sports. "I was a Communication major. I had no idea what one did with a Communication degree, and I really didn't care because I'd received a track and field scholarship and I had to major in something. What it was didn't matter to me. I planned to compete in the Olympics."

"The Olympics, Olympics?"

She nodded, and he gave a low whistle.

"That's major."

"Yes. Which is why I was devastated when I tore my ACL to sherds the summer before my Junior year." It was a long time ago, and though she no longer experienced the overwhelming sense of loss she did at one time, it still hurt a bit when she looked back on that time.

"I can't even imagine how difficult that was." He both looked and sounded sincere and she couldn't help but feel sad she was only just seeing and talking to the real Evan. Not only that, but she was enjoying herself as well. Why now after all this time was she just seeing there was more to Evan than his handsome face and teasing ways? She had been an idiot and a half to have never once even tried to look beyond the surface he showed.

It wouldn't do any good to look at what might have been. She'd had the last several years to get to know Evan and now it was too late. There wasn't anything either of them could do now this late in the game.

And that was a damn shame.

Chapter Four

Two Months Later

WILMINGTON, Delaware

KELLY WOULD BE LYING if she said she hadn't been counting the days to Julie and Daniel's wedding. When she originally accepted the job in Texas, she'd never have thought that would be the case, but there you had it; she missed Delaware.

Although not necessarily the city itself. More specifically, she missed her friends. She told herself it was to be expected. She'd lived in Delaware for years and the friendships she'd made here couldn't be replaced overnight. There were several people she'd met in her first few months in Dallas she could call 'friend' and hopefully one day, they'd be as close as her Wilmington friends.

But there was one big difference. Most of her friends in Wilmington she'd met at the Partner's group. She had yet to attend a BDSM group meeting in Texas. Not for lack of looking, but none of the groups she found online seemed to be anything like the one she left behind here. It was possible she was being too picky but she didn't think so.

It was Saturday afternoon, and she'd arrived back in town late the night before. Too late to call anyone, and to be honest, there was only one person she gave serious thought about calling when she made it to her hotel room past midnight.

And she'd left her phone alone. Even though they had exchanged a few text messages over the last few months, her exchanges with Evan had never gone any deeper than the high level, 'how are you' sort. For all she knew, Evan had a plus one he'd bring to the wedding today.

She'd picked out the dress she'd wear to the nuptials with care, telling herself she didn't care what Evan would think of it, but knowing she wasn't fooling anyone. In the end she bought a pale pink, form fitted dress with a flared skirt. Times past, he'd tease her mercilessly whenever she wore her favorite color. She wasn't sure what bozo decided that redheads weren't supposed to wear pink, but he could stuff it. Evan could as well.

Right, you want him to stuff it all right, as deep as he can into you while you beg him to never stop.

Please. She was a Domme. She didn't beg for anything. Especially from a man.

Technically, you're a switch.

She hated it when she argued with herself. Shutting down

26

her inner voice, she turned her attention to the front of the church.

Less than three minutes later, the processional started. Julie had asked Sasha to be her maid of honor; Abby, Dena, and Julie's sister stood up with her as well. Dena's husband, Jeff, was the best man, Cole, Nathaniel, and Daniel's brother-in-law rounded out the wedding party.

With everyone else in place, and Daniel standing at the front of the church looking happier than Kelly had ever seen, the congregation stood and turned to face the back door in anticipation of Julie's entrance.

But before her gaze settled on the spot where the bride would appear, it met the warm blue of Evan's stare. In the seconds before he, too, turned to wait for Julie, Kelly couldn't help but notice there didn't appear to be a plus one in the picture. With a self satisfied smile, she focused her attention on her two friends getting married.

An hour later, everyone had moved to the clubhouse for the reception. Abby and Sasha saw her enter and immediately made their way to her.

"When did you get in?" Abby asked, grabbing her in a hug. "I hadn't heard anything from you and feared you wouldn't come."

"Please. I've been waiting for this wedding for years. Nothing was going to keep me away." Kelly took a step back and looked at Sasha. "And how are you and Cole doing? You're next, you know?"

"Yes, but we're going much less formal and we aren't inviting near as many people."

Sasha and Cole lived as Master and slave. It wasn't a lifestyle Kelly had any interest in, but she'd known Sasha for as long as she'd known Julie and the petite brunette had never looked better or been more in love and as content as she was in her current relationship.

"Sure,"Abby replied. "That's what all brides say."

"But I mean it."

Abby remained silent but sent Kelly a *yeah right* look.

Sasha didn't appear fazed at all. "Tell us what's new with you. How's Dallas? Met anyone interesting?"

"Dallas is great. I love having my family nearby, and police work is police work, but no special man so far," she said, knowing that was what Sasha really meant with her question.

"That transparent, am I?" Sasha asked with a giggle.

Kelly smiled, it was so refreshing to see Sasha happy and laughing. "Pretty much."

Sasha changed the subject to Julie and Daniel's wedding, and they all agreed how perfect the bride and groom were for each other, and how beautiful Julie looked.

"Excuse me, ladies," someone said from behind them and Kelly's breath caught at the sound of Evan's voice.

Though all three women turned, Evan only looked at Kelly. Her heart raced. She'd not remembered just how blue his eyes were. The time apart from him had done nothing to diminish the effect his nearness had on her.

"Kelly," he said. "Will you dance with me?"

Abby and Sasha gasped in unison. Kelly turned

automatically to the nearby dance floor. While she'd been chatting, the number of couples dancing had increased to where they filled almost all the space. Her mind raced to find a reason to turn him down: she didn't dance, the song was too slow, there was no room.

But she didn't want to turn him down, and the truth was she didn't know why she was trying to come up with reasons to do so. No, the truth was she wanted to be in his arms and feel his body pressed against hers.

Her gaze fell to his outstretched hand and she placed her own in it. His thumb caressed the top of her hand and her stomach fluttered at his whispered, "Thank you."

They walked to the dance floor and Kelly wasn't sure if it was her imagination or not that the room fell silent for a millisecond before the soft hum of conversations picked up again.

Evan stopped at the edge of the dance floor and took her into his arms.

Oh, God, this was such a mistake.

She liked the feel of his arms way too much.

She liked the heat of his body way too much.

She liked the mischievous grin he wore way too much.

"I expected you to show up today in a cowboy hat and boots," he said, and instead of shooting back with a retort of her own, she laughed.

Hell, she liked the way he teased her way too much.

"I'm not that much of a Texan," she said. "I did live in Wilmington for a number of years, you know."

"True," he said. "But I found I couldn't joke about you wearing pink today because you look so damn hot and I had to tease you about something."

She sucked in a breath. He thought she looked hot? *In pink?* With a shake of her head, she decided not to reply with a snappy comeback. If he could control himself and not joke about her wearing pink, surely she could likewise keep the smartass replies under wraps.

The song ended and neither one of them made a move to part ways. *Well, this is certainly different.* She kept her eyes focused on Evan's chin, not wanting to see her old friends' reaction at her and Evan dancing.

Evan had one arm around her waist and held her hand with the other. She leaned further into him when he pulled her closer. "It seems we're causing more than one open jaw stare," he whispered in her ear and her body shivered, though she wasn't sure if it was a result of what he said or the fact that his warm breath tickled her skin. "We were fairly inconspicuous until Julie pointed at us and said something to Daniel."

She groaned. "And I can't even say anything to her because she's the bride."

Evan chuckled and her belly tightened in response because that chuckle made his body brush against hers in several awesome ways.

"You have to admit," he said. "If it hadn't been her, it would have been someone else."

"True, but no one else is the center of attention today other than her."

"No one else *was* the center of attention," he said.

She forced herself not to look. "What? Who else would anyone be looking at?"

"A certain redheaded siren in a pale pink dress."

"Please. I'm the most boring person here."

He didn't say anything, and for some reason, she got the impression he was angry. But about what?

"Are you okay?" she asked.

He remained silent, and she assumed whatever had pissed him off wasn't her business and would stay that way.

"If you were my submissive and said something like that, I'd punish you," he said, breaking the silence. "I find it hard to believe you would allow your subs to do that either."

What the hell was he talking about? "I have no clue what you're yammering on about," she said.

His body didn't relax, but remained ramrod stiff. "You talking down about yourself. You said you were the most boring person here and not only is that not true, but you're putting yourself down. I don't allow it from my submissives and I'm sure as hell not going to allow it from you."

Her heart threatened to beat right out of her chest. Fuck, the thought of his hands on her in punishment. She took a shaky breath, determined not to let him know how much his statement turned her on.

"You think you can discipline me?" she asked in her best Domme voice.

He pulled back a touch and captured her gaze. "I suggest

you don't start down a road you're not prepared to reach the end of."

His gaze was so intense, even if she wanted to look away from him, she wouldn't be able to do so. "What does that mean?"

"I think you would allow me to do a good number of things to you."

He was right and even though she wasn't going to lie and tell him otherwise, not that he'd let her get away with lying to him, she didn't want to agree with him, either. Instead, she said nothing.

And of course, her silence didn't bother him at all. He leaned close and she made herself stay still and not move back. "I'm not sure if you don't remember or if you're only pretending you don't." His voice was low and seductive, and she never wanted him to stop talking. "It's possible you don't remember, you were quite sloshed, after all. Or maybe you think it was a dream and never happened, but let me assure you, it did. You told me you never fucked the men you topped."

She'd told him that? Fuck. What else had she told him? She started breathing heavier and he smirked. Damn, she hadn't thought he'd be so observant. Which was stupid on her part, because he was a Dom and from what she'd heard in the women's locker room, he was a good one. She should know better than to think she could keep something like that from him.

"So you tell me, Kelly. Do you fuck other men or has it been that long since you've fucked?"

She tried to pull up the outrage to at least pretend to be

offended, but found it impossible to do so. However, she couldn't speak because her mouth was too dry. She licked her lips and his breath hitched.

She got some self-satisfaction from that and smirked herself as she replied,"It's been that long since I've fucked."

As she thought, he hadn't expected her to actually answer, much less to answer the way she had. Someone nearby cleared their throat and Kelly jumped back, looked up, and discovered not only had the song ended, there was no music playing at all and almost everyone was looking at them.

Feeling her face heat, she turned away from Evan and walked off the dance floor, trying to act as if it was no big deal she just been caught by all the guests at Julie and Daniel's wedding talking about how long it'd been since she'd had sex. Regardless if anyone heard or not. She wished she was a chameleon with the ability to blend into the background. But even as a chameleon, such a thing wouldn't have been possible with the way Evan stopped by her side on his own way off the dance floor and whispered, "This isn't over."

It might not be over, but she wasn't going to make it easy for him. Hell, she wasn't even sure she wanted to talk with him anymore. For the rest of the reception, she kept her distance from him, though she'd be lying to say she didn't monitor him. Not that it mattered, she caught him keeping track of her.

Whether or not they admitted it, and whether or not they liked it, there was something that drew them to each other.

They could fight it all they wanted, but it would always be there.

Kelly thought about drinking a little too much again, but found she couldn't do it. After Daniel and Julie had their big farewell, she walked past Evan on her way to leave. But she stopped after taking only three steps away from the front door. She wouldn't wait long, but she would wait for a few minutes. No more than five.

She didn't have to wait two, and she appreciated he didn't attempt to cover that he'd followed her out.

"I was hoping to catch up with you before you drove off." He stepped right into her personal space without apology and brushed his fingers down her arm. There was no way he didn't notice the gooseflesh his touch left in its wake. "I didn't want to leave things the way they were between us."

"You and I discussing my sex life, or lack thereof?"

"With you and I at odds." He dropped his voice and the rough tone revealed more than he probably planned. "Let's go somewhere private to talk."

An outright lie if she ever heard one. If they went anywhere private, there would be no talking. They were both sober, and the awareness between them only intensified every time they were together.

She didn't care. "Come to my hotel room."

His eyes flashed with raw lust and need, but his voice was calm when he replied. "I don't want to be something you regret."

"You already were."

Chapter Five

"You already were."

Kelly's words echoed in Evan's head, even as he followed her car to her hotel. He'd been so surprised by her answer he hadn't questioned her about what she meant. What exactly did she regret? Moving? Or that the two of them had never got together before she moved?

He hoped she didn't mean what they were getting ready to do in her hotel room. They were both adults who were attracted to each other. They had bickered with sexual undertones for years. Neither of them thought they would end up in her room drinking coffee and chatting. She knew as well as he did once they were in that room together, all bets are off. The past was past. The future hadn't happened yet. There was only now and it would be them, naked and fucking, and nothing else.

He had wondered if she would show up at the wedding. At first it didn't look like she would make it and he'd been afraid she wouldn't be there. But he knew how close she was to both Daniel and Julie, and that nothing short of an emergency would keep her away. Sure enough, he only had to be patient. She walked in wearing that light pink dress and looking fucking gorgeous. He barely kept his eyes on the ceremony in front of him. After a few minutes, he didn't even bother trying to concentrate on anything else. He knew all he would think about was Kelly.

Or more to the point, Kelly in that pink dress. How it would feel to take it off her body. Inch by inch. Slowly revealing the skin underneath. Like he was unwrapping the biggest fucking present of all time.

He pulled to a stop at a red light, while Kelly continued on to the hotel. She'd told him where she was staying, as well as the room number, so he didn't feel the urge to catch up once the light turned green. He shifted, attempting to ease the discomfort of his erection and finally gave up, knowing nothing would work. Nothing except sliding it deep inside Kelly, and telling her to hold on while he rode her good and hard.

Fuck it, he couldn't wait.

But when he'd parked at last and made his way to her room, he knew they couldn't do anything until he found out what she meant at the reception when she claimed he was already a regret. Maybe he was being shortsighted or stupid. Maybe it didn't matter why he was a regret as long as they were able to correct it tonight.

And maybe it didn't matter if they could correct it or not.

He took several deep breaths while standing in front of her door, hoping to calm his dick down. They would talk, damn it, before they did anything. Even though he'd wanted her for years, he also respected her and needed to know where she'd been coming from with those words.

Decided, he rapped on her door with his knuckles and took a step back, closing his eyes and repeating in his head what he would say once she opened the door.

"You don't know how much it means to me that you asked me to your room tonight. I've wanted you for years, and to know you feel the same is a fantasy come true. However -"

"Are you going to stand there all night or are you going to come inside?"

His eyes flew open at the sound of Kelly's voice. She stood in the doorway, looking at him as if he was the last piece of steak at an all you can eat meat buffet. Normally, he bristled at being viewed as a piece of meat, but tonight, she could grill, fry, or flambé him and he wouldn't complain a bit. Actually, he wasn't sure if meat flambé was a thing, but whatever.

He opened his mouth to tell her he wanted to talk for a few minutes, but she grabbed him by the collar of his shirt and pulled him inside while at the same time somehow managing to both kiss him and close and lock the door behind him.

Fuck. It was better this way, anyway.

He moved, wanting to get a hand on her ass, but she pushed him against the wall and lifted his arms so they were over his head. Pulling back she caught his eyes.

"Keep them here," she said.

He didn't have to. After all, he was both bigger and stronger than she was and she hadn't bound him. But she had a raw sexual energy about her and damn it all, he wanted to see what she did with it.

"Say please," he said because teasing her was so much fun.

She cocked her head to the side. "That's not how I work."

He kept his hands where she'd put them, but he wasn't ready to completely comply with her. Or at least he wasn't ready to let her *think* he was. "Then you can look at this as a chance to learn a new way of doing things."

He expected one of her typical snappy comebacks or at least a hint of challenge in her eyes, but she gave him neither. In fact, the set of her lips and the way she held her head sent a message that she expected nothing less than his obedience. "That's not going to happen either."

"What makes you so certain?" Raw sexual energy aside, did she really think he'd do everything she asked without any pushback?

"It's really very simple. All you have to do is ask yourself one question." She cupped his erection. "Would I rather be a smartass or have Kelly's mouth wrapped around my dick? Because you can't have both."

That certainly explained the confident look, because fucking hell, she was right. "I'll keep my hands here all damn night in that case."

This time she laughed softly. "I thought you'd see things my way. Or at least a certain part of your anatomy would."

There was no reason to argue with her. Especially when she was one hundred percent correct. "I normally don't allow my dick to make decisions for me, but it seemed prudent in this case."

"It did, did it?" she asked and this time he didn't answer. He couldn't because after she ensured she'd captured his eyes again, she sank to her knees before him and he discovered he'd lost the ability to speak. "Move your hands and I stop. Got it?"

He nodded.

"Words, Evan," she said. "You know better."

"Yes," he ground out. "I've got it."

She didn't say anything else, rather, she adjusted her position slightly and undid his pants, sliding them down his legs and bringing his boxer briefs along with them. He sucked in a breath as the cotton slipped over his too sensitive cock.

"Damn, K," he said and then stopped because at that moment she engulfed nearly his entire length in her mouth, and he forgot what he was going to say. "Holy. Fucking. Shit," was all he managed to get out.

He'd had plenty of blow jobs in his life. High School girlfriends. College girlfriends. Assorted dates. Newbie subs. Experienced subs. No one had ever rocked his world the way Kelly did. For one, she didn't seem to have a gag reflex. For another, she did something with her tongue every time he thrust forward and it felt like nothing he'd experienced before.

As much as he tried to hold out, her mouth made it impossible. Still it was only good manners to let her know.

"K," he said. "I can't hold it back much longer. If you don't want to….." His voice trailed off as one of her hands inched toward his backside and one of her fingers pressed into his ass. His world exploded in a flash of pleasure. "Fuck!"

Several seconds passed before he could move, but when he looked down, Kelly had sat back on her heels and was licking her lips. His dick twitched, wanting more.

"You didn't move your arms at all," she said as he realized the same thing. "Impressive."

He allowed them to drop to his side and he winced while working a few kinks out of them. "Practice," he said. "I've asked subs to do the same thing and if I'm going to ask them to do it, I should at least now what it feels like and at best, be able to do it myself."

She licked her lips again. "Everything?"

"I see what you're doing now," he said to her, as seriously as possible.

"You do?"

"Yes," he said. "You're trying to kill me. Payback, I suppose, for the hell I've given you over the last few years. The thing is, I don't even care. I'll die a happy man."

"Oh yeah?"

"Yeah. With a smile on my face and the memory of my cock in your mouth." He closed his eyes and leaned back against the wall with his arms tucked behind his head, making sure his smile conveyed total bliss.

She smacked his chest and snorted. "You are so full of it."

"Where did you learn how to do that so well?" Because seriously, the woman had mad oral skills.

"The blow job?" At his nod, she continued, "I took a

course." He raised on eyebrow. "More like a series of courses."

"Really?"

"Really," she repeated. "We started with Cock 101 and went all the way through Resurrection: Bringing the Lifeless Back to Life with Fellatio."

He stared at her for a handful of seconds, not wanting to believe her, but damn if she hadn't spit it out like there actually was a course series. "I don't believe you. You didn't take any courses."

"No, I didn't. I'm a Domme and I want to be able to properly reward the subs I play with. It behooves me to know how to give a great blow job." She lifted an eyebrow. "Just like I'm sure you know a thing or two about how to eat a pussy."

Damn straight he did. He grinned. "Only one way for you to find out."

She took a step back, shaking her head. "I didn't mean it like that."

He advanced on her. "Mean it like what?"

"Like you had to reciprocate."

She'd stopped moving backward, so that was a good thing. He knew he hadn't misread any signs, but if she kept moving back, he had no choice but to take her actions as a no. "Trust me," he told her, hoping beyond hope that she believed him. "I've thought of little else than what your pussy would taste like. In fact, you'd actually be doing me a favor, you know, to see how correct I was about how good you'd taste."

She rolled her eyes. "Seriously? Does that line work for you?"

"I'm not sure," he said with a grin. "I've never used it before. Ask me tomorrow how it goes."

"You're something else, you know that don't you?"

"I'm nothing special," he admitted. "You know that as well as I do. All I am right now is a guy who wants you. A guy who wants to reciprocate the pleasure you just gave me by giving you some of your own."

"I didn't do what I did just so I could have you do the same to me."

He lifted his hand, not sure if she'd let him touch her, but wanting to try all the same. She didn't move when he touched her cheek, so he lightly stroked it with one finger. "I know that," he said. "And because of that, it only makes me want you more."

She closed her eyes and seemed to lean into his touch.

"Let me do this," he pled. "Let's go into the main room where you can get on the couch and I can get on my knees and taste you."

He had to refrain from sending up a cheer when she gave a curt nod, turned and walked to the center of her hotel room. She settled herself on the couch but didn't do anything else.

Could it be she was waiting for instructions or something from him?

From all appearances, that seemed to be the case and he didn't want to be the one who didn't give her what she was asking for.

"That's it, Kelly," he said. "Now that you're on the couch, I want you to slide down a bit so your ass is at the very edge. Hike that skirt up around your waist. I don't want anything between your pussy and me."

She hesitated before following his directions and it only took less than half a second once she'd lifted her skirt above her hips, baring her body to him from the waist down, for him to see why.

"Look at that," he said. "Someone was a dirty girl at her friends' wedding. Someone didn't wear panties."

"Trust me, I did. I took them off once I got back here."

"Even better. Someone wanted to be a dirty girl, but only for me. Is that right?"

She nodded.

"Does that also mean someone wanted to sit with her legs spread wide while I tasted her greedy pussy?"

Kelly moaned. "Fuck, yes."

Of course, her admittance of that in no way turned her docile and compliant. He didn't expect it to. However, he also didn't expect her to take matters into her own hands. Yet, she did.

She licked one finger before dropping her hand between her legs, teasing her folds, and dragging one finger across her seam. Her eyes stayed on his while she fingered herself. He supposed it was her way of reminding him she was submissive to no man, but he needed no such reminders.

"That's right," he said. "Show me how you like it. Let me see what turns you on. That's it. Get yourself nice and wet for me while I watch and learn all your secrets."

Her eyes widened in disbelief as if she didn't think that was what he was doing. He smiled.

"You think I'm sitting here watching a show?" he asked. "Hell, no. I'm gathering every scrap of information I can about what makes you tick so when I get my hands on you, I'll pleasure you so thoroughly, you won't be able to move without thinking about me. I like to think of you sitting there in front of me as my own private series of courses called How to Properly Fuck Kelly. And believe me when I tell you, these are courses I plan to ace."

He stopped talking for a few seconds to let all that sink in. "Let me know when you're ready for me. We'll see how fast I can make you come with my mouth." He stroked his cock. "And since watching you has made me hard again, maybe once I make you come with my mouth, I'll fuck you nice and proper." Making sure he had her attention, he gave a powerful thrust into his hand. "Although, I have to be honest, there won't be anything proper about me once my cock is buried deep inside you."

Kelly dropped her hands and grabbed on to the couch the best she could. "Do it," she said. "Use your mouth to make me come."

"I thought you'd never ask." He took his time getting to her, enjoying the way she watched him, her eyes bright with anticipation.

Once he made it to the couch, he stood between her legs, a hand on each of her knees and pushed them open more. "Wider," he said, bitting the inside of his cheek to keep from saying 'good girl' when she obeyed. "Now, place one of your hands on each knee, and don't move."

She mumbled something under her breath as he knelt

where he stood, pleased to find it a good position.

"Damn," he said. "This is one hot pussy. I need to cool it down before going any further." She twisted this way and that, trying to get an idea of what he had up his sleeve. He took a deep breath and blew a long stream of air across her sensitive skin that sent her writhing in pleasure.

"Oh, yes," he said ensuring he kept close enough for her to feel the heat from his mouth as he spoke. "That was a lovely reaction. Let's see if I can get you to squirm like that again."

He did so, not once, but over and over until she was panting with need.

"Please, Evan."

"Please, Evan, what?" He blew across her skin, light so she wouldn't come, but enough that she'd give him what he wanted.

She let out a string of four letter words. He laughed. "Try again."

"Please, Evan. Touch me and make me come."

He flicked his tongue across her clit and she came with a yelp. "Nice," he said, before she could gather herself together and try something similar on him. "Now you're going to come again."

This time, he put his mouth on her the way she probably thought he would from the start. He tasted her, and whispered how delicious he found her. He parted her with his thumbs and licked her until she cried out and came for the second time.

"There you go," he said. "If you come one more time, I'll

let you have my cock."

"You'll let me have it?" she asked, obviously more aware of things than she'd been following her first orgasm.

"Yes," he replied. "It is *my* cock, after all. I believe I do have a say in who gets it and where."

Instead of arguing with him, she wisely changed the direction of the conversation. "You're going to try and make me come a third time? And you plan on only using your mouth?"

He propped up on one side so he could see her better. "You say that as if it's impossible."

She shrugged, all traces of the passionate woman pleading for her release that he had his hands on moments ago were gone. "Not impossible," she said as if telling him it would be mostly sunny tomorrow. "Just improbable."

He wasn't sure if she was stating a fact or issuing a challenge. Most of the time, like now, she kept her emotions under wraps and it was difficult to get a read on her. One of the reasons why he wanted her to come again was because when she was consumed with pleasure, all of those wrappings fell away, and it was just her. Kelly.

Whether she meant it as a challenge or not, didn't make a difference. He said she was going to come again before she got his cock and that's what he meant.

"At least once more," he said. "I suggest you get back into position and hold on nice and tight to those knees."

She looked at him as if he lost every bit of sense he ever had, but she did as he asked. "I have to check out by eleven o'clock tomorrow morning, you know."

Chapter Six

As her heart rate and breathing returned to normal following orgasm number four, Kelly realized that of course Evan took her statement as a challenge and not in the *hey-just-so-you-know* kind of way she meant. She thought she was helping his male ego by letting him know before he got started that rarely did she come more than twice a night and he shouldn't take it personally.

Instead, he decided to prove her wrong. Not that she was complaining. Hell, no. Not after experiencing the complete and total domination of his mouth. Talk about courses, though, that man could get rich teaching the skills he had. And while she'd truly expected him to brag about his pussy eating power, instead, he'd said nothing. Which in a lot of ways was worse.

Worse because she knew he was probably wondering what duds she'd been going out with lately that had no clue as to what they were doing. The thing was, there were no duds of any kind. It'd been ages since she'd been on a date, much less had someone put his face between her legs.

Evan stood up and held out his hand.

"What?" she asked, still feeling a bit high from her last orgasm.

"I thought it might be nice for us to move to the bed for the next part."

She happened to glance down at that moment and saw his cock. He was hard and ready, and to be honest, the sight of him made her want to spread her legs and beg him to fuck her. If he was that talented with his mouth, wouldn't it stand to reason he would be likewise talented with other parts of his body?

She might not live through a night with his cock inside her, but she'd die happy and content.

When they made it to the bed, he surprised her by pulling her close and spinning them around so she was on top, one of her legs on each side of his body.

"What?" she asked, having pegged him as a missionary man.

"I would have thought it obvious." He placed his hands on her waist. They'd both finished undressing between orgasm three and four, so there was nothing in their way at this point. "You've been living in Texas for months. Show me what you've learned. Ride me, Kelly."

"I live in Dallas. It's a major city, not a ranch."

His expression was filled with mischief. "I've been jerking off for two months to the thought of you on top of me, your tits bouncing, my cock deep inside you. I'm the wild stallion you want to tame, to bend to your will. You ride me as hard as you can, using my cock for your own pleasure. You think you have me mastered, but the truth is, I'm not bucking in an attempt to get you off of me. I'm doing my damnedest to get just a little deeper inside you."

It never crossed her mind he'd be such a dirty talker, and frankly, she liked that he was. That was the thing about Evan, what she had noticed after being in the Partner's Group for so long. He flew under the radar. Several of the Doms, Cole and Nathaniel were the first two coming to mind, you felt their presence before you saw them. Their domination evident for anyone who looked. It was entwined with their personalities so tight, they couldn't hide it if they tried.

Evan, however, was what she'd call a quiet Dom. Not that there was anything remotely quiet about him. His Dom side wasn't what one first took notice of. In fact, she wondered if he ever showed it outside of a scene? No, it was only when he'd drawn you in with his good looks and his wicked sense of humor you realized there was more to him than what he showed the world.

Like right now, looking at her with eyes filled with desire, and surprising her by asking her to ride him. He was one hundred percent walking and talking sex. From the look on his face, he knew it, too.

"Here," he said, holding out a condom. "I'll let you do the honors."

Her hands trembled slightly. Just a result of the four orgasms, she tried to convince herself, but she didn't believe it even as her mind told her it could possibly be true. *No, it couldn't.*

Her hands were trembling because she knew what was going to happen next and she wanted it so badly. She'd had that cock in her mouth and she could only imagine how good it'd feel inside her. She made quick work of the condom, ripping it open and rolling it on his hard thick length.

He hadn't seemed quite as large before, but all his size did was make the empty parts of her ache to be filled. She stroked him after the condom was in place and he groaned low in his throat. The rough sound sent shivers of anticipation down her spine and she stroked him again.

"Fuck, Kelly," he said. "Keep that up and this will be over before it has a chance to get started and I don't think either one of us wants that."

She thought about making a joke with his use of 'keep that up' but she didn't want to start a verbal spat. What she really wanted was him inside her. "If you insist," she said and lifted her hips and moved over his cock.

She lowered herself on him, head thrown back, letting herself get lost in the feeling of him. How big he felt. Shit, forget that. How big he *was*.

"Look at me," he insisted.

She looked down, thinking it'd be awkward, but instead it was one hundred times hotter. This was Evan she was in bed with. He was the one inside her; the one who filled her up so completely. Evan of all people. Her nemesis for years. The man who had teased her mercilessly about everything from the way she spanked to the fact that she liked to wear pink.

He lifted his hands to cup her breasts and ran his thumbs

across her nipples. She groaned when he gave them a pinch.

"Harder," she urged, squealing in pleasure when he did so.

"Fuck, look at you." He thrust his hips upward in time with her downward movements, making his way deeper and deeper inside her. "I knew you'd be perfect."

But the truth was she was far from perfect. And not only did she live in Dallas, but they were both Tops. There was no possibility for any type of relationship after tonight.

"Hey," he said, rolling her nipple between his fingers. "Where did you go?"

"Nowhere." She smiled, determined not to let thoughts of tomorrow ruin what they had tonight. If they only had this one night, she sure as hell wasn't going to spend it doing anything other than him.

"I'm not sure I believe you, but I don't want to fight while I'm fucking you and you feel so good." The grin appearing on his face was the exact same one he always had before one of their verbal spats. "Know what that means?"

"I'm afraid to ask," she replied, thinking this surely had to be the most bizarre conversation she'd ever had in the middle of sex. Not that she typically had conversations in the middle of sex.

"I'm going to have to work harder to keep you here with me instead of wherever it is you went inside your head." He abruptly pulled out of her and slapped her upper thigh. "On your hands and knees."

"Excuse you?"

"You heard me, I want you on your hands and knees."

It should be ridiculous him standing there with his cock as hard as it was, telling her to move to her hands and knees. Should be, but it wasn't.

The truth was, she never much liked being on top during sex. It made her feel way too exposed and as if she was somehow being judged on her performance. Being on top messed with her mind and she'd never once had an orgasm in that position.

Hands and knees, however, was her favorite. If she was going to come from fucking, it would happen in that position. Plus, she always felt tighter that way, and as much as Evan filled her while she was on top, she bet it would be one hundred times better on her hands and knees.

"Such a brute," she couldn't stop herself from saying as she rearranged herself into the position he asked and that she was most comfortable in.

He slapped her ass this time. "It's the way you like me and you know it."

She didn't even attempt to deny it. Not only did she like it, she rather liked the way he spanked as well. Another thing she'd never tell him, not for a million dollars.

Evan placed himself at her entrance and every thought flew from her head except how good he felt thrusting into her the way he was. The assumption he'd feel even tighter had been correct.

"You feel so good," he half groaned and with a powerful thrust, went deeper than he had before. "So good."

He fucked her in a hard and unrelenting rhythm, pounding into her like she only existed for that reason. No man had ever been that way with her before. They'd treated her reverently, too gentle, as if she couldn't handle or meet the demands of a hard cock and an equally hard fucking.

But not Evan.

He treated her the way she wanted to be treated, like he couldn't take his next breath without being inside her and only doing so on his terms. He somehow understood that she didn't want or need to be treated with kid gloves. She was a grown woman, strong enough to know her own mind and he respected that.

Likewise, he was a grown man, strong enough to fuck like one.

And boy did he.

"Come with me," he said, his voice choppy, but he never once slowed down. One of his hands brushed downward, trailing the curve of her ass. She assumed he'd rub her clit the way he'd done earlier.

Which is why when he brought his hand down with hard spank on that sensitive area, her climax nearly blinded her. He followed quickly, holding still while buried deep inside her.

She waited for him to roll over, sit up, and get dressed in order to go back to his own house. But he surprised her by putting his arms around her and pulling her close.

"I'm going to dispose of this condom and unless you object, I'm going to come back to bed."

"I'd like that," she said, the words spilling out easily.

"Thank you." He pressed a kiss to the back of her neck and crawled out of bed.

She must have dozed off for a few seconds. The next thing she was aware of was of him crawling in next to her. Somehow her arms came up and looped around his neck. "Stay," she heard herself say.

His chuckle was warm against the skin on her shoulder. "There's not a snowball's chance in hell I'm going anywhere."

Chapter Seven

He woke with a start, shocked at how bright her room was, though he shouldn't have been. After sleeping for a few hours, he'd been tugged from his slumber by the feel of her mouth on his cock. Three more orgasms, one for him and two for her, and they'd fallen onto the bed for a few hours rest, still holding each other.

While they'd been sleeping, she'd untangled herself from him and rolled so her back was to him. He took the few private moments he had to watch her while she slept. She was naked and the sheet had slipped off of her at some point during the night. Positioned the way she was, only one breast was covered. The uncovered one had a red bite mark on it.

The submissives he played with typically liked it when he left a bite mark or a bruise on them. But Kelly was a Domme and he wasn't sure what her reaction would be. Frankly, he liked it. He wasn't sure if she'd joined a BDSM club in Dallas or not, but it satisfied some primal male urge in him to have marked her. At least temporarily.

Although he had to admit the chances of anyone seeing the mark, other than the two of them, were slim to none. He and Kelly had belonged to the same BDSM group for years and in all that time, he'd never once seen her topless.

No, the only way someone would see that mark is if Kelly was fucking him and he knew her well enough to know that if she had a lover back in Texas, she wouldn't have slept with him last night. At the moment she was single.

The same primal male urge liked that as well.

In fact, that part of him liked it so much, he wondered if Kelly would be interested in some sort of long distance relationship. After the way they'd spent the last ten hours or so, he couldn't imagine her not wanting to at least consider something of the sort with him.

True, they both led busy lives, but everyone else did as well. If they wanted it bad enough, they would be able to make it work somehow. He had some money put away and, if she was agreeable to the idea, he'd be able to fly to Dallas occasionally. He resisted the urge to grab his phone and check flight prices. But really? How expensive could it be?

He worked on a chart in his head, with weekends set aside for them to get together somewhere. It could be in either Wilmington or Dallas, but it didn't have to be. They could always meet somewhere between the two.

Also, since he taught high school, he had most of his summers free. While he normally attended local enrichment classes, wouldn't it be infinity better to fly to Dallas and spend a few weeks with Kelly?

He couldn't wait for her to wake up so they could discuss their options.

As it turned out, he shouldn't have been in such a hurry for her to wake up, after all. Oh, it was fine at first. The slow way she opened her eyes, the somewhat hesitant smile she gave him upon realizing he was still in bed with her. Though, that should have been his first clue the long distance thing wouldn't go over well with her.

"Morning," she said, glancing over his shoulder to look at the clock behind him. "Wow, I can't remember the last time I slept in so late."

"Probably because we didn't get to sleep until the early morning hours. It's not like you ended up getting a lot of quality sleep."

Her cheeks flushed at his reminder of how they'd spent the hours before sleep. It was unexpected and quite lovely.

"True," was all she said in response.

It was her hotel room and she probably had to check out in a few hours. He should get up and leave so she could do whatever it was she needed to take care of before flying back to Dallas.

That was what he *should* do.

But it was not anywhere at all close to what he wanted to do.

Instead, he lingered in her bed, watching as she leisurely sat up, realized she was naked and pulled the covers up. He couldn't help but smile at the sight of her being so self conscious after everything they'd done together the night

57

before. He'd not only seen every inch of her body, he touched and tasted every inch as well.

"What time does your flight leave today?" he asked.

She didn't look at him as she rose from the bed. "One forty-seven."

"I guess you'll need to be heading to the airport soon. Can I buy you breakfast first?" His gaze settled on the clock. "Or brunch?"

"I appreciate what you're doing, but there's no need. I knew what I was getting into last night when I asked you here."

She might as well have thrown ice water on him. "What is that supposed to mean?"

"I'm back in Wilmington for the weekend, to attend the wedding of two good friends. Now that it's over, I'm going back to Dallas." She didn't sound angry, only resolved, but either way, it wasn't how he expected the morning to go.

"What exactly are you trying to say, Kelly?" He tried his damnedest to keep his voice calm and even, but he failed.

"I'm going back to Dallas today," she said like he was dense and one, didn't understand the words the first time she said them seconds before, and two, somehow didn't know she was going back to Dallas today to begin with. "We are not a thing. Never have been. Never will be."

He wasn't sure what pissed him off more - that she'd assumed he wanted more than the night they'd shared or that he actually did and she'd shot him down.

"Damn," he said. "I was only offering to buy breakfast. It's not like I proposed or anything."

"It's not like you're some stranger I picked up at a bar to scratch my libido's itch with. I knew who you were when I asked you to come over, and when I opened the door to let you in."

"I'm sorry, but I still don't know what this has to do with breakfast."

"You don't do morning after breakfast."

"What the actual fuck?"

"Do you think the Partner's submissives don't talk to me or even around me because I'm a Domme? Think again. When we're in that dressing room, we're all just women, and the number one thing women talk about is men. So yes, I know your morning after routine. And I know you don't do breakfast."

On one hand, he couldn't argue with her because she was right about the whole breakfast thing. But seriously, is that what they did in the dressing room? Sit around and talk about guy's morning after habits?

"You disappoint me, Kelly," he told her. "I'd have expected more of a group member with your experience. I honestly didn't have you pegged as a silly gossip girl."

"You think I care for a second what you think about me? Think again. I don't give a fuck about whether or not you approve of my behavior when I'm chatting with friends. All you were was a good lay to begin with. A cock to get myself off on."

She snatched a piece of her clothing off of the floor, shot him a nasty look, and stormed past the bed to get to the bathroom. He wasn't sure, but he thought she might have damaged the entire doorframe based on how hard she slammed the door once she made it inside. Surely she'd at least put a crack in it. Within seconds, the water to the shower cut on. No doubt she was washing away anything having to do with him.

He pulled on his own clothes as quickly as possible, not wanting to be in the room when she came out of the bathroom. Stuffing his shirt into his pants, he tried to think back on anything that could halfway explain what was wrong with Kelly this morning. Any action on his part. Anything he may have said, even inadvertently. He couldn't find one thing or word. Sure they had exchanged words over the years, but it had all been in fun.

The same could not be said about the words spoken this morning. Not a one of them had been said in jest. No, she had been going for blood, and she got it. Unwanted, her words echoed in his head. *"All you were was a good lay to begin with. A cock to get myself off on."*

How had he read everything so completely wrong? He'd been planning long weekends together while she was counting down the minutes until he left. No, breakfast wasn't on his normal morning after routine, but Kelly wasn't the normal woman he took to bed. All he knew was that when he woke up, he wasn't ready to say goodbye to her yet. Neither of them had eaten anything since the wedding. The way he saw it, he'd get to spend more time with her and eat at the same time. Win - win for everyone.

Should he have told her that? Would it have done any good?

He didn't think so.

KELLY STAYED in the shower until her fingers wrinkled. Even when she got out, she listened intently to ensure no sound came from the other side of the door. She didn't think Evan would have stayed around for her to get out of the shower, but she had to make sure.

She wanted to burst into tears when she thought about the words she'd forced herself to use. The things she'd said to him. Ugly. Hateful. Cruel. Even worse had been his expression when she told him he'd only been a cock she got herself off on. Before today, she wouldn't have thought it possible for her to think such things, much less to say them.

Standing in the hotel bedroom where she'd passed the best night of her life, she wanted to do nothing more than to chase after Evan and tell him she hadn't meant a word of what she said. He'd believe her, she was certain. She'd make sure he believed her.

Her cell phone buzzed and she automatically turned her head to look. That was all it took to remind her *why* she'd acted so out of character this morning. The phone's display still showed the text from her sister she'd seen as soon as she woke up. Before Evan realized she was awake. Only two words, but they were enough.

He's out.

Now, a missed call was also displayed. She didn't recognize the number, but she knew the area code and that was enough.

Chapter Eight

It was dark by the time Kelly pulled into her sister's driveway. The entryway light was on since she'd sent a text when her plane landed so she'd be expecting her. The one thing she hadn't done was call, deciding face-to-face would be better.

Kelly parked her car and walked to the front door, casually scanning the area to ensure nothing was out of place. Her sister lived in a quiet neighborhood, one of a hundred just like it in the Dallas area. For the last few years she'd been working as a nurse at a local school after deciding she didn't care for the hospital setting.

Though Kelly thought it had to do more with the fact she'd broken up with one of the top neurosurgeons around the time she left the hospital.

The blinds in one of the front windows moved as Kelly reached the landing. A quick glance showed no evidence of security cameras. Looked as if she'd be doing some shopping sometime in the near future.

She was certain her sister knew who it was, or more importantly, who it wasn't, at her door, but just in case, she shot off a text and knocked on the door. "Kiara," she called. "It's Kelly."

The blinds moved again and then came the sound of footsteps down a hardwood hallway. Kelly took a step back as the door cracked open half an inch.

"Kelly?" her sister asked.

"Yes. It's me." The door opened wider and Kelly stepped inside and gave her sister a big hug. "It's going to be okay. I'm here now."

KELLY AND KIARA were fraternal twins, but no one ever seemed to hear the fraternal part. The reply was always, "Really? You don't look alike at all."

True enough. Where Kelly was petite, curvy and red headed. Kiara was tall, slender, and had beautiful light brown wavy hair that Kelly had been insanely jealous of growing up. As an adult, she'd grown to like her hair, but had to admit it was nice living in Delaware where no one ever called her, *You know, the redheaded one.*

And even though they had their physical differences, they were alike in other areas. They both worked in public service, neither one of them could sing a note to save her life, and they both had a less than stellar track record with the opposite sex.

But as Kiara cried on her shoulder after ensuring the door

was relocked, Kelly had to admit her sister's track record was worse. Which was saying a lot considering Kelly's last twenty-four hours.

She led Kiara to the living room so they could both sit on the couch. "Tell me everything."

They had gotten together several times since Kelly's return to Texas, but because of one reason or another, they'd never had the time for a face-to-face and heart-to-heart talk. In fact, Kiara had said nothing to Kelly about anything having to do with a man. It was only because Kelly was living with her parents while she both worked and house hunted that she knew anything.

Her parents had said Kiara had been in a relationship with a man they didn't get along with but it was fine because he was in jail now. That was it. They didn't get along with him and he was in jail. Kelly had pressed for more information, but it was useless. Either they didn't know or they weren't telling.

It wasn't until the weekend before the wedding that Kelly was able to dig up any dirt. But she was here with Kiara now and planned to hear the entire story.

"I'm so sorry," Kiara started. "I know you had that wedding this weekend and you were in Wilmington. But I heard that Randy was out on parole and I panicked. I knew mom and dad had to have told you and I was so afraid he'd come by here first thing."

"All I heard from the two of them was they didn't like him but it was okay because he was in jail." Kelly snorted. "Nice to know that can land you jail time here."

As she hoped, Kiara laughed. "Unfortunately, it's not. He was found guilty of animal cruelty."

"That doesn't sound good at all," Kelly said, which might possibly be the understatement of the year. "Start at the beginning."

A little over a year and a half ago, Kiara had met Randy online after growing tired of her girlfriends hounding her to set up a profile. Several men had responded, but there was something in Randy's that set him apart from the others.

"That sounds really stupid, doesn't it?" Kiara asked her. "Looking back today, I can't even tell you what it was. It wasn't anything specific he said, I guess it was the way he used words. I don't know. All I do know is that once I read his, I didn't bother with anyone else."

For the first three or four months, everything had gone well. He treated her like a queen, got along with her friends, and had a killer sense of humor. Other than her parents not liking him, life was great.

Or so she thought.

It wasn't until five months or so ago that one of her friends complained that it'd been nine months since they got together.

"I told her she was batshit crazy," Kiara said. "We went out all the time, but when I looked at a calendar, I realized she was right. Randy and I had been going out, but only with his friends. That was when I woke up."

Kelly kept her expression neutral. She'd heard similar stories before, but unfortunately, most of the time, women didn't see what was happening until it was too late. Kiara was one of the lucky ones.

It happened so gradual and seemed so natural, Kiara hadn't thought anything about it. Randy's manipulation of her life had been so meticulously orchestrated, even an uninvolved third party would have trouble seeing it for what it was.

"I couldn't believe it. Or more to the point, I didn't *want* to believe it, but when I looked at everything, how he'd isolated me from my friends and family, how deliberate he'd been in slowly expanding my personal boundaries? Nothing else made sense."

Unfortunately, Kiara had underestimated how possessive Randy felt about her.

"When he came home that night, I told him I'd been thinking and thought it would be for the best if we saw other people."

Without hesitation, Randy punched her hard in the stomach and when she doubled over in pain, he'd grabbed her hair, jerked her head up to force her to look at him, and calmly said, "No, I don't think so. What's for dinner?"

Kelly sat frozen in rage. In fact, she found it hard to breathe. "Tell me where he lives," she managed to get out. "I'll kill the mother fucker myself."

On second thought, killing was too easy on him. She'd castrate him with her bare hands and *then* she'd kill him.

"No," Kiara said. "I can't let you do that."

Kelly raised an eyebrow. "Why the hell not? Please don't tell me you still think you're in love with him."

"Oh, hell no," Kiara said. "I hate him. If I ever see him again it'll be too soon. And I'd like nothing more than to rid the world of him myself, but I can't and you can't either."

"Give me one reason."

"Because if you kill him, it'll ruin your life, and he's not worth it."

"No, he's not." Kelly took her sister's hand. "But you are."

They talked late into the night. Thankfully, Kelly was off until Tuesday and the summer school Kiara worked at was out for the week.

However, Kelly couldn't get Kiara to tell her why Randy got arrested for animal cruelty or if he ever hit her again. Kelly could dig around at work and find the answer to the first question, and she assumed Randy had struck Kiara again, simply because she'd never heard of a one-time only abuse situation. But there was no official reason for her to be digging into Randy's case. She could have gotten away with it in Wilmington, but she was still too new in Dallas and didn't want to press her luck.

While Kelly was fine with Kiara keeping those details to herself, there was one thing she would not compromise on. She would move out of her parent's house and in with Kiara, and as soon as she could get it scheduled, Kiara's house was getting a security update. Surprisingly, Kiara didn't argue with her about either, which spoke volumes about how freaked out she was over Randy.

<hr>

THE MONTHLY PARTNER'S group meeting was the last place

Evan wanted to go tonight. The main reason being it would be the first time since the wedding, two weeks ago, he'd be seeing most of the group members, the majority of whom witnessed his departure from the reception with Kelly. He didn't want to think about that weekend, much less talk about it. He'd considered not attending, but he didn't want to give Kelly's memory that much power over him.

She'd called him once. He recalled staring at his phone and thinking he must be seeing things as her number flashed on the display. By the time he realized it actually *was* her, she'd disconnected and hadn't left a message. He almost called her back to see what she wanted, but ended up not doing it. If she wanted him to call her back, she'd have left a message or sent a text.

He finally told himself it was a butt call.

He'd already decided how questions about their time together following the wedding would be answered. *None of your damn business.* Now he only had to say it without sounding as if his world had fallen apart.

With a sigh of determination, he opened the door of his car and headed into the newly constructed building. If he'd timed it right, he'd have just enough time to find a seat and sit down, thereby putting off any Kelly questions until after the meeting.

"Right behind you," a man from behind him said in a distinct British accent.

Evan held the door open for Cole and Sasha, greeting the beaming couple as they entered. Now that Daniel and Julie were hitched, the Master/slave couple were next in line to get married. End of August if he remembered correctly.

Evan should say something about their upcoming nuptials, but at the moment, weddings were the last thing he wanted to talk about.

"How's your summer going?" Cole asked him as they all three made their way to the front desk to check-in.

Apparently Evan hadn't been the only one with the idea to arrive just in time. He'd never seen a line so long to get in. But at least if he was talking to Cole, he wouldn't have to answer any questions about Kelly. Cole wasn't into gossip or knowing everybody's personal business.

Sasha, however, was a different story altogether. Not that she was a gossip, but as a friend of Kelly's, he couldn't say with any certainty the Domme's name wouldn't be dropped in conversation. The only thing that might work in his favor was Cole usually instituted high protocol for Sasha during group meetings, which meant she wouldn't be able to talk to Doms without Cole's approval. Evan knew the couple well enough to know when permission had been granted and she didn't have it yet. Not to speak with him any way.

"So far the summer's been pretty dull," Evan said in answer to Cole's question.

They moved up a step in line, and Evan was almost ready to call it a victory with regards to no questions about Kelly when Sasha spoke.

"Sir?"

"Yes, little one," Cole replied, and you'd have to have a heart made of ice not to smile at the way he looked at the woman who wore his collar. Sasha whispered something, and Cole lowered his head. "Of course," he said when she finished whatever it was she wanted to tell him.

But when Cole lifted his head, he looked at Evan.

Shit.

Cole lifted an eyebrow, and Evan wondered if he'd spoken out loud. "Sasha wanted me to ask you if you've spoken with Kelly lately, and if so, how's the situation with her sister?"

There was a situation with her sister?

"Judging by the look on his face, little one," Cole said. "I'd guess the answer is 'no' and that he was unaware there was a situation in the first place."

Evan was stuck. He couldn't say now that he knew what Sasha was talking about. It was doubtful Cole would fall for an, "Oh *that* situation." But if there was a situation with her sister, he wanted to know. *Damn. Why hadn't he returned Kelly's call?*

The answer to that one was clear. Pride.

He hadn't wanted to appear weak and he'd incorrectly thought that if he called her back, he'd look weak. Like he'd been waiting by the phone for her to call.

"I would never disrespect you by lying," Evan said and, at Sasha's cough covered snort, hastily added, "Well I might, if I thought I could get away with it. But I wouldn't, so it doesn't matter." He took a deep breath. "No, I wasn't aware of a situation with Kelly's sister. Things didn't end well for us after the wedding. I'm still not sure exactly what happened, but I did have a missed call from her and if something's wrong with her or her sister, I'd like to help if there's a way I could."

They had reached the check-in desk, so they paused their conversation until they finished and entered the main portion of the club. Cole led them to a lounging area where no play was permitted, and away from the crowd heading toward the meeting. The sitting area had numerous chairs, lounges, and sofas that could be arranged in numerous ways. Cole selected an area with several small sections. He sat on a love seat and Sasha gracefully sank to her knees on the soft rug at his feet. As was typical whenever Evan had observed them in the past, Cole's hand went straight to Sasha's hair. Under her Master's touch, Evan watched as Sasha's body relaxed, but he was surprised when he removed it after a few seconds.

Evan decided he hadn't covered his shock very well when Cole chuckled. "Yes, I did stop sooner than normal. Sasha would actually sink into subspace if I continued, but I know she's anxious about Mistress K, so I thought it best not to get her there quite yet."

"Sorry, I didn't mean anything by staring." The fact was, Evan had never been interested in a twenty-four, seven power exchange. However, after witnessing how in love Cole and Sasha were and how effortless everything about them appeared, it made him think there was more to it than he'd previously thought.

"No need to apologize," Cole assured him. "Sasha and I are quite used to quiet observation from those who know how we live but have never experienced it themselves."

"How about those who don't know how you live?" Evan asked.

"You mean society at large?" Cole asked and Evan nodded. "Like if we're going into the city, perhaps we have tickets to Broadway? What are our seating arrangements?"

Evan felt a bit abashed he asked anything until he saw the glare Sasha gave her Master.

"Sorry, little one," Cole said. "I couldn't help it. Forgive me?" Only when she nodded, did he turn back to Evan. "She didn't want you to feel bad for asking. Apparently not everyone appreciates my sense of humor. But the thing is, I think she's actually the one to best address that question. We recently went out to dinner with her brother and his girlfriend when they traveled to the city to do some shopping. We'd never met the girlfriend, and I've only been around her brother a handful of times. He is strictly vanilla and has no idea about the kinkier side of our relationship."

Evan nodded. He didn't even have a sister and he understood why that would be.

"I honestly didn't think much of it until he called her a few days after they returned home to Dover." Cole shifted his attention to Sasha and stroked her cheek. "I'll let you tell Master Martin how the conversation went, little one."

Sasha turned her body so she rested against Cole's legs while looking at Evan. "It was actually rather sweet," she said. "My brother said he wasn't going to bring any more dates around us until we cooled it down a bit."

Evan wrinkled his forehead. "Cool it down a bit? Haven't you and Master Johnson been together for years? How long does he think it'll take?"

"We've been together a little over two years," Sasha said. "What makes his comment even funnier, is when you

73

realize he and his girlfriend have been together even longer."

Evan nodded, but he had to admit he knew what her brother meant. Cole and Sasha, whether they knew it or not, and he had a feeling they didn't, seemed to have this air about them. It wasn't that they were overtly sexual, and it wasn't anything he believed them to be conscience of. If he had to give a word to define it, he would say there was an awareness between them. An awareness so strong one could sense it even when one of the two stood across the room from the other.

Evan had known Sasha for longer than he'd known Cole, and in all that time, he never seen her look at anyone else the way she did Cole. He was happy for them. For them both as well as hopeful for himself that maybe one day, he'd be in a relationship with such an awareness.

"Back to you and Mistress K," Cole said. "I'm sorry you learned the existence of the situation from us, but I don't believe either Sasha or myself feel comfortable disclosing information of that sort without Kelly's approval."

"I understand, Master Johnson." To be honest, Evan hadn't expected him or Sasha to do so.

"I will say, however," Cole continued, "That a missed phone call is just the type of sign I'd be looking for. Maybe if you call Kelly back, she won't be opposed to telling you more."

Chapter Nine

Evan ended up not calling Kelly. Though all the reasons Cole had given him at the club made sense at the time, when he made it back to his place that night, he found they no longer did. Kelly was a smart woman and had no trouble knowing her own mind from everything he'd ever observed. She had his number, and if she didn't want to talk to him, she could always text. Besides, if she didn't want him to know about whatever was happening with her sister, he wasn't going to put her into a position where she felt like she had to tell him.

He changed into a pair of shorts and a tee. For some reason he felt out of sorts, maybe a jog would help clear his head. He reached for his running shoes, and his phone rang. His heart sped up. Maybe it was Kelly, but when he looked at the display, it wasn't her and he didn't recognize the number. Most of the time when he didn't know who was calling, he didn't pick up, yet for some reason, he felt he should answer this one.

"Hello?" he answered.

"Evan?" a familiar male voice asked, but he couldn't place who it belonged to or where he might know it from.

"Yes," he answered. "Who is this?"

"Man, I can't believe it's you. It must have been six or seven years." Now that whoever it was spoke more than one word, Evan could hear the faint southern accent. It hit him suddenly that Kelly didn't have one when she talked, and he wondered off-hand why that was.

The man on the other end of the line had kept talking, "Couldn't believe she knew you. Damnedest coincidence I've ever heard of, much less experienced -"

"I'm sorry," Evan interrupted. "Did I miss you saying who are?" He hated to be a pain in the ass, but seriously.

"Sorry, man. It's Orson Kent."

"Orson?" he asked in a half laugh because with the name came back four years of all the crazy shit they did in college.

"Yeah. Hard to believe, isn't it?"

"You can say that again."

Randomly put together as roommates their freshman year, they had hit it off instantly and ended up living together for four years. Though they had different majors, they spent most of their time together when not studying, in class, or with a girl. Or with a girl they weren't sharing, he clarified in his head. Perhaps, not surprisingly, they had both discovered their Dom nature while in college.

Orson had grown up in North Carolina, but vowed he

would never live there. Indeed, after graduation he'd moved to Nevada with plans to open a high end hotel/conference center marketed to the kink community. He'd asked Evan to come and invest with him, but Evan couldn't see moving across the country for a business deal that might not pan out. Especially when Delaware would help in paying off his student loans in exchange for him teaching.

Maybe one day he'd be in a position to where he could do something uncertain like that, but at that moment he had to be smart. So even though he'd have loved to throw caution to the wind and move to Nevada, he did the sensible thing and decided to teach high school. But he'd always wondered how different things might have been if he'd gone with Orson.

"Are you still teaching?" Orson asked.

"Yes," Evan replied. "How's the kink community in Nevada?"

"It's actually Texas now."

"What was that?" Evan asked, he thought he heard him say Texas, but he had to be mistaken.

"I sold the business in Vegas," Orson explained. "I've bought a place in Texas."

Evan was so shocked he found himself unable to speak at all. Not that it mattered, Orson kept right on talking. "What I like about the Texas place is that we're family friendly Monday through Friday morning, and kink friendly Friday night through Sunday."

Evan still couldn't get any words to come out. *Texas? What the fuck was Orson doing in Texas?*

"It's nice to have some variety, you know?" Orson paused. "Are you still there?"

"Yeah." Evan coughed. "Where exactly in Texas are you?"

"We're outside Houston."

Evan let out a deep breath. Not Dallas. He'd been expecting him to say Dallas, though he wasn't sure if he was happy or sad when he didn't. "Sounds like you have a nice place. Maybe one day I'll make it dow there."

"Funny," Orson said. "I was just going to ask you a favor."

⊙⊛⊙⊛⊙⊛⊙

"Why are you only now telling me this?" Kelly didn't even try to hide her irritation. No need to do so when she was fairly certain she had smoke coming out of ears.

"Because I knew you'd be like this." Kiara wiggled her fingers at Kelly. "But the main reason is I forgot."

Kelly sighed. If she was talking to anyone else, she wouldn't believe it possible to forget, but when the person in question was Kiara, that changed the equation altogether. Although, part of her still found it difficult to believe her sister conveniently *forgot* that a week from now, once the current summer school session ended, she'd volunteered to work at a destination type ranch as a nurse until school resumed in the fall. Kelly didn't care if she'd signed up last summer and only remembered when the ranch sent her a welcome email, there were some things you just didn't forget.

"I'm not sure how you expect me to keep you safe and provide security for you when I'm in Dallas and you're in

Houston." Though, technically speaking, the ranch wasn't in Houston. It was forty miles away and yet somehow still considered to be on the outskirts.

"And see, when I remembered I'd volunteered, I thought being out of Dallas and in Houston was a positive."

"How did you come up with that?" Kelly asked. "The way I see it, you'll be hundreds of miles away and I won't have the ability to get to you fast."

Kiara chewed her bottom lip. "Randy doesn't know I volunteered, he won't know where I am, and that'll drive him crazy."

Kelly appreciated her sister at least thinking through the potential consequences of her actions. However, it seemed as if she only thought of the positive ones and or chose to ignore the negative ones. Which was fine if you wanted to avoid reality, but unfortunately Kelly's job didn't give her the luxury of only seeing positive outcomes. Of course, she would have thought the same thing about Kiara's job.

Kelly wished she'd thought through the consequences of her tirade with Evan. If she had, things would have ended very different. It was doubtful she'd have said any of the things she had. She'd actually called him a week ago, and had written out everything she'd wanted to say to make sure she didn't forget anything once he was on the phone. But he hadn't picked up, and when his voicemail clicked on, she froze, not having thought through leaving a message. In the end, she'd hung up.

Like she had any room to criticize Kiara for doing the same thing.

Kelly shook her head, as if she could shake Evan out as

well, but no such luck. It wasn't that easy and that was fine, he could stay there. He just couldn't occupy too much space at the moment because she had to focus on keeping her sister safe.

"You running off and heading out of town will only be safe for you if he doesn't follow you or have someone else follow you and report back to him."

Kiara face went deathly white at Kelly's words. "Shit, do you think that's what he'll do?"

"I'm not sure, but he might and that's why I have to think about all potential outcomes." Kiara had filed a restraining order against him, but Kelly knew all too well that if Randy wanted Kiara, a piece of paper wasn't going to stop him.

Kiara nodded, her face still paler than normal. "If he comes after me at the ranch, I'll have a ton of cowboys I can let loose on his sorry ass."

"True enough," Kelly agreed but didn't voice her thoughts. She'd have a ton of cowboys if they cared enough to take on a fight that wasn't theirs. But it could just as easily swing the opposite direction. "But regardless, I'll be the one driving you to the ranch next Saturday, so I can make sure no one's tailing us."

Kiara whispered, "Thank you," and pulled Kelly into a tight hug. "What would I do without you?"

"I hope you never have to find out," she replied back, blinking back tears. "Because I plan to stay around for a long time."

. . .

THEY LEFT EARLY the next Saturday. Kelly didn't have to report into work until Wednesday and she planned to spend her free days checking out the ranch as thoroughly as possible. If she could get away without being too obvious, she also planned to talk to as many ranch employees as possible. Also, she knew for a fact Kiara hadn't mentioned anything to the owner of the ranch because Kelly had asked her straight out. 'Talk with ranch owner' was also on her rapidly expanding To-Do list.

The four hour drive passed quickly and Kelly pulled into the ranch's long driveway feeling better than she had when they'd started out. No one had followed them, she was certain. It wasn't until she breathed a sigh of relief and the tension left her back and shoulders, that she realized she suspected someone would have at least tried.

She'd never been more happy to be proven wrong. Kiara must have picked up how Kelly's mood had improved because you'd have to be blind not to notice her twin's smile.

"All clear?" Kiara asked.

Kelly hated to put a damper on her sister's happiness, but it wouldn't do her any good to be lulled into a false sense of safety. "All clear for now," Kelly added. "The only thing we know is that I don't think anyone followed us today. That doesn't mean he's clueless about where you are or that you shouldn't still be on alert."

"Got it," Kiara said and pointed at a man walking toward the car. "I think that's the owner, Orson Kent. Just so you're aware, I called him last night and filled him in on what's been happening with me as well as who you are and a little bit about what you'd be doing."

Kelly couldn't help but raise an eyebrow. As far as she knew, her sister rarely took the initiative to do anything of the sort. Especially since Kelly had asked her about it yesterday morning and Kiara seemed to have no plan to tell the owner anything.

"Don't look at me like that." Kiara crossed her arms. "He called to make sure I didn't need anything or have any last minute questions and I told him everything. Well, almost everything. What can I say? He's easy to talk to."

Kelly could see that as soon as he came into view and made his way to them. He was very easy on the eyes, with a smile that would probably put the most ill at ease to rest. Not to mention his boy-next-door good-looks.

"The Ms. Bowmans," he said, holding his hand out. His hair was tucked under a cowboy hat, of course, but here and there a few wisps had found their way out. Enough to show his brown hair. She couldn't say anything about his eyes since he wore shades, but his voice was warm and welcoming. "I'm Orson Kent."

"Kiara Bowman," Kira said, shaking his hand.

"So happy you're here, Ms. Bowman."

"Call me Kiara."

Orson Kent had a very nice smile. "Thank you, Kiara." He turned to Kelly. "You must be Officer Bowman."

"Kelly," Kelly said and shook his hand. "We have a lot to discuss. Let me know when you're free."

"Give me about ten minutes and I'm all yours. In fact." He pointed at the closest building to them. "This is where both of you will be staying. Let me find someone to carry your luggage inside and we can talk. If you'd like, you can await for me in my office." This time he pointed to the building on the far right. "First floor. Can't miss it."

She didn't want to leave Kiara alone, but she told herself that was stupid and her sister was safe here. She shot Kiara a questioning look and received a nod in reply.

"What are our room numbers?" Kelly asked Orson.

He gave her a set of keys. "I put you both on the first floor with rooms next to each other. You're one eleven and Kiara's one thirteen."

"You have my bag?" Kelly asked Kiara with one glance to make sure she was alright. But Kiara only had eyes for Orson. "Kiara?"

Kiara waved her on. "I'm fine. I promise. See you in a bit."

And just like that her sister dismissed her, once more turning her entire attention to Orson. The man in question gave Kelly a look that seemed to say, "I've got this all under control." To be completely fair, it did seem as if he could handle just about anything that came up. He had a look about him similar to those she'd seen on men who'd been in the special services. Strong. Determined. Totally in control. Oh yes, Kelly was willing to bet Orson knew every inch of his property and would put the beat down on anyone who was stupid enough to attempt to try to take or harm anything he saw as his.

She took her time walking to the building where Orson's office was located. He was helping to get Kiara settled, after all. It wasn't as if he would be sitting inside waiting for her. She knew about the ranch from a combination of both Kiara and online research she'd done on her own.

Though Kiara had eventually told her about the kinky weekend side of the ranch, Kelly had read about it first online while visiting a forum she participated in occasionally. From all accounts it was highly regarded, and Orson had a stellar reputation as both a businessman and a Dom.

Though today was a Saturday, she knew from what she'd found online that this was a no-play weekend. It also meant she and Kiara probably weren't the only ones moving in. Especially since in the welcome packet it stated that tomorrow would be filled with training. Before arriving she hadn't thought about attending but now she thought it might be a good idea for her to do so. If for no other reason than to get a good feel as to who everyone was.

She made it to the front of the building Orson had indicated housed his office, and from there she could see the expanse of the property. Also visible was the obvious division between weekend and weekday properties. Separated by a large building she assumed held the kitchen and dining rooms, to the left were a handful of weekend buildings, while to the right were numerous and varied ones for weekday use.

Kelly turned to open the front door and instead, ran headfirst into a man exiting.

"Sorry," she said. "Wasn't looking at where I was going."

The man was silent, giving no, "it's okay," or, "watch where you're going," or even, "what the fuck?" She looked up to see what his problem was and she gasped.

"Evan?"

Chapter Ten

Evan had to be seeing things. He shook his head to dispel the image of Kelly standing in the entrance of the office building he was leaving.

"Evan," the hallucination said, and he realized he'd never heard of hallucinations speaking before.

"Kelly?" he asked just in case he hadn't lost his mind completely and she really was standing there.

"What are you doing in Texas?" she asked, and he knew she was real because if she'd been a hallucination of his, that's not the question she'd want the answer to.

"I think the better question is why you think you should be privy to my travel schedule? Maybe if you had called or sent a text sometime I would have mentioned it."

He expected her to argue. He was prepared for her to argue. Instead, she agreed with him and threw him off his game.

"You're right. I should have reached out to you somehow." She blinked, and for a second before her lashes came down, he could have sworn he saw tears in her eyes. "But I didn't," she continued, "because I was ashamed. Though I actually did call you once."

So it wasn't a butt call. He tried to tell himself it didn't matter. "Doesn't count if you don't leave a message."

"I know," she said, sounding defeated, and he fucking *hated* for her to sound that way.

He opened his mouth to ask her why she'd called him, but at that moment, Orson walked up.

"Evan. Kelly," he said, taking his glasses off. "I see you two have met."

"We've actually known each other for years," Kelly said. "I recently moved to Dallas from Wilmington."

"Is that so?" Orson asked with a glance toward Evan. Was he asking if Kelly told him the truth? Evan wasn't sure why he would think she was lying.

"Yes," Evan confirmed. He didn't tell Orson Kelly was a Domme or anything of that nature. Evan didn't know why Kelly had been hired or what information she offered about her sex life, if anything. The only thing he knew with any certainty was no one would hear confidential information from his mouth.

Orson paused for a minute as if he thought by waiting for long enough, Evan would spill the beans or something.

Not going to work, old friend. You forget I've been a Dom for just as long as you.

"Evan," Orson finally said. "Why don't you join the two of us in my office?"

Evan raised an eyebrow, trying to figure out what the man was up to. Although it didn't really matter, he wasn't ready to walk away from Kelly. An invite to Orson's office gave him the opportunity to stay with her and hopefully to see what Orson had up his sleeve. If nothing else, maybe he'd figure out what Kelly was doing here in the first place.

"Best idea I've heard all day," Evan replied and, since he was closest to the door, held it open for Kelly and waved her through. "After you."

Kelly narrowed her eyes as she walked by and it caught him off guard until he put himself in her place and saw what the situation might look like from her point of view. Did she think he'd somehow been in contact with Orson, found out she was working here, and then invited himself to Texas?

He almost brought up how he hadn't talked with Orson since forever, and how they were college roommates, but the more he thought about it, the more it sounded like he was only making excuses for being here. And that wouldn't do. He didn't need an excuse to be here. Hell, he'd agreed to come help Orson for the rest of the summer without knowing Kelly was even in the picture.

Would he have said yes sooner if he'd known? Of course, but what did that have to do with anything? The fact was, they were both here now and they'd both have to deal with it.

He couldn't help but eye her ass as she walked in front of him. No matter what, she had a damn fine ass.

"Which office is his?" she asked, turning around and catching him. "Are you looking at my ass?"

"Last one on the right, and yes."

He expected her to call him a name. That's what the Kelly he knew in Wilmington would do. But he was beginning to suspect that Kelly in Texas was slightly different. Maybe because of whatever that situation was with her sister? Who knew?

He should still be angry after the way she was the morning following Daniel and Julie's wedding. He shouldn't even want to talk with her. But that was a lost cause. He'd long suspected something had happened that morning without him knowing and it had spurred her to act the way she did. The very fact she wasn't acting pissed at the world proved to him that he was right. At least on some level.

Having been in Orson's office recently, Evan knew what to expect when he stepped inside. Two walls were covered from floor to ceiling in books. Evan remembered Orson telling him in college that growing up he was so poor, he was never able to have books. The rows upon rows now decorating his office spoke to how hard he'd worked to overcome his past.

A third wall was made entirely from windows and showed why his friend had claimed this office as his instead of any of the other ones. Sitting at his desk, Orson had a view of almost his entire ranch if he looked out the window.

Pictures covered the forth wall. When he'd arrived a few days ago, Evan had looked over the photos. They were all of families who'd stayed at the ranch. Orson, like him, had never married and had no children. Evan knew from college that also like him, Orson was an only child.

Across from Orson's big wooden desk sat two leather chairs. They were large and overstuffed, and Evan remembered how he'd almost fallen asleep in one of them shortly after his arrival when he'd been chatting to catch up with Orson.

Kelly took a seat in one of the chairs.

There was no way in hell he'd fall asleep today. Not with every cell in his body acutely aware of Kelly sitting mere inches from him. Man, he was some kind of fucked up to still want her the way he did after how she'd treated him and what she'd said to him the last time they were together.

"I have to say." Orson tossed what Evan recognized as his and Kelly's employee files on his desk and took a seat. "Even knowing you were both from Wilmington, it didn't occur to see which club you were both at until just a few minutes ago. Daniel Covington and the Partners Group?" He shook his head. "What a crazy coincidence. I met Daniel years ago. Probably would have caught it sooner but I had someone else do your security screening, Evan, since I know you."

Kelly cut her eyes to Evan.

"We were college roommates," Evan told her. "Four years."

Kelly laughed. "Figures. My sister decides to get a part time summer job working for the one Dom you know in Texas. Seriously? What are the odds?"

"To be fair," Orson said. "Evan didn't know I was in Texas until a few days ago."

She raised an eyebrow.

89

"Before he bought the place here, he was in Vegas. That's where I thought he was."

Silence fell over the three of them. Evan was getting ready to ask Orson if he really needed to be here when his old friend spoke again.

"Kelly," he said. "I assume nothing's changed and you'll still only be here on weekends?"

Only on weekends? What the hell?

She nodded. "Unfortunately, that's the case. I haven't been with the Dallas PD long enough to have vacation days."

"That's fine," Orson said. "By any chance does your sister know Evan?"

"No." She shook her head. "They've never met."

"Hmm." Orson seemed to be thinking her reply over. "My idea should still work, but let me run it by the two of you."

Basically, Orson planned to have Evan serve as Kiara's watchdog. He would follow her during the week, and they'd both have immediate and direct twenty-four, seven access to the ranch's security team. It was his belief that with Kiara and Evan starting at the ranch around the same time, no one would question them pairing up.

Evan clarified Orson only meant pairing up and not hooking up. He did.

Also, Orson added, Evan didn't have the typical bodyguard build, and as a result if anyone was watching, Evan's presence wouldn't be considered suspicious. The same couldn't be said if Orson used a man from his security detail.

Evan snorted and said he wouldn't take Orson's words personally. "Besides," Evan added, "I know you wouldn't use me if there was any doubt in your mind that I could kick major ass if I needed to." He didn't wait for Orson to confirm before turning to Kelly. "I would like to know details about the threat against your sister if you don't mind me knowing."

"No, of course, not," Kelly assured him.

She proceeded to tell him about Randy, the way he'd manipulated Kiara, drew her away from her friends and isolated her, and how he hit her once that Kiara admitted. Evan agreed with Kelly's intuition that it'd more than likely happened again. She ended with the animal cruelty charge and Kiara's fear he was looking for her.

"Let him try to get to her while I'm anywhere nearby," Evan said. "I'll make sure he only ever sings soprano." He couldn't help but notice as she spoke that Kelly acted a bit guilty. Noticeable because she didn't have anything to be guilty about where Randy was concerned.

If it wasn't Randy she felt guilty about, what else could it be? Was it possible it had something to do with her time in Wilmington for the wedding? And if so, maybe she felt at least a little bad about how they'd left things?

He watched her closer as the meeting went on with Orson; studied her body language. It wasn't his imagination or wishful thinking on his part, he caught her glancing his way and more than once. Her eyes never stayed on him for long, but he'd have to be dead for it not to affect him.

She still wanted him.

Oh, she could try to deny it and he had no doubt she

would. But the one thing she couldn't lie about was how her body reacted to him. The way she leaned, more than likely subconsciously, whenever he shifted toward her. The way she licked her lips. Even the subtly seductive way she'd push a strand of hair behind her ear, her fingers lingering and then tracing over skin he'd touched and tasted not too long ago.

Skin he had all intentions of touching and tasting again.

Orson asked him a question and Evan realized he hadn't heard a thing the man had said in the last five minutes. "Run that by me again," he asked his old friend.

"I asked if you thought it was a good idea for you and Kelly to touch base during the week since she'll only be here on the weekends?" Orson repeated with an eye roll. "Maybe a quick call at the end of the day and a debrief when she arrives on Fridays?"

Evan wasn't sure what Orson was up to, and his expression didn't give anything away. If he and Kelly spoke every night would they really need a weekly debrief?

Was he really going to argue about spending alone time with Kelly?

Hell, no.

"Sounds good to me," Evan said with a nod to Kelly. "If she's okay with it."

"It's a good place to start," Kelly said. "We can always change it later if we see the need."

Orson stood up. "That's that, then. Evan, I know you've only been here a few days, but would you mind giving Kelly a tour around the place?" He looked at Kelly. "I'll go and make sure Kiara is settled and let her know you'll meet up with her later."

Yup, Evan wasn't sure, but Orson was definitely up to something. This was only made more obvious with how he wouldn't meet Evan's eyes, and the way he walked off after dismissing them. However, if Kelly noticed anything, she didn't show it.

"Ready for the grand tour?" he asked her.

Chapter Eleven

Evan had shown Kelly about half of what he'd planned to before she started talking.

"I appreciate you doing this," she said. "I know the way I acted in Wilmington probably didn't leave you with a burning desire to help me."

They had walked through the daily areas of the ranch: the rooms for the weekend and weekday guests, the common areas, and the dining room. Now, he'd turned them toward the barn and outbuildings. Orson had told him both her room number and Kiara's. She probably assumed his room was close to hers, but she'd be wrong. He was staying in a caretaker's cottage near the barn.

"You know, I could be a real ass and ask you what makes you think I'm doing any of this for you," Evan replied, doing his best to keep his voice even and jovial, but at the same time to let her know he hadn't forgotten anything about that weekend.

"You could," she agreed. "But I think we both know between the two of us, I'm the bigger ass, especially where that weekend is concerned."

He couldn't argue with her about that, so he didn't attempt to. Instead, he leveled his gaze at her. "As true as that statement might be, I know the real you and it's not the woman I woke up to that weekend. My only regret is not calling you on it and forcing you to tell me what the hell was going on."

"I'm not sure you could have gotten me to tell you."

They passed the barns, and he didn't even mention them. She didn't seem to find anything strange about that, so he kept going, bringing them to the cottage he was staying in. "You underestimate me," he said, opening the door and waiting for her to enter. "I can be very persuasive when I need to be."

She looked around the tiny but cozy living room. He'd loved it on sight and for some reason, he wanted her to see it, to see if she felt the same.

"What is this place?" she asked.

He took at step back, needing to see her expression. "It's where I'm staying this summer."

She looked up, wearing a mild expression of shock. "Here?"

"Yes."

"Why did you bring me here?" There wasn't an accusation in her question, but rather a curiosity.

"Maybe I wanted to test my powers of persuasion on you."

"Oh?"

He moved toward her this time. Only a step, but she would know what he was up to. "You and I both know that one night wasn't nearly enough to satisfy whatever this thing between us is."

She didn't move away, didn't deny his words.

"Tell me, Kelly," he said. "Tell me you don't want to explore it more. Tell me you haven't got yourself off thinking about how good we were together. Give me anything, a word, a sign, a gesture, anything to tell me you don't want this, that you want to go back to the main campus, and I swear we'll leave immediately. Tell me you want nothing to do with me, and I vow by all that I hold dear, I won't bring it up again."

She stood silently, watching him, but not saying anything. Doing nothing to refute anything he'd just spoken.

"You can't do it, can you?" he asked.

"You know I can't."

He closed the distance between them until there was no space left and he could feel the soft tremors within her. He lifted her chin and forced her to meet his eyes. "You want this? You want me?" Because, damn it, he was going to make sure there was no doubt at all tonight.

"Yes, please, Evan." Even if she hadn't said the words, her eyes told him exactly what he wanted to hear. But then she said, "I'm so sorry I said what I did. I've felt so bad about it," and he knew beyond a shadow of a doubt what he had to do next.

Even though every cell in his body rebelled, he made himself walk away and sit on the couch. "I appreciate you telling me how sorry you are about that weekend, but as you well know, sometimes words aren't enough." And just in case there was any confusion in her mind about what he wanted, he patted his lap. "Come here."

"You have got to be kidding me."

He hid a smile from her. "I kid about a lot of things as you're well aware, but I never kid about punishments. Strip from the waist down and get over my lap. I'll only use my hand, but by God, Kelly, I will spank your ass for the way you acted."

She struggled. He could see it on her face. Part of her wanted to obey and part of her balked. "I'm a Domme. You can't spank me."

"We both know I can. But I won't without your consent. However, since you are a Domme, I know you understand why this needs to happen before we move forward."

"Oh, shit," she said, but her voice was low and raspy, and he imagined arousal pooled between her thighs.

"Now, Kelly. Over my lap so I can spank you nice and hard the way you deserve."

"But, it's going to hurt."

"Damn straight it's going to hurt. You were rude and ugly and you lied. Don't you think you deserve a spanking that hurts? Do you honestly think you need anything less than my hand turning your ass nice and red, giving you the spanking of your life?"

He'd probably pushed her too hard. He truly expected her to turn and walk away. But she didn't. In a voice so soft, he had to strain his ear to hear, she said, "Yes, Sir. That's what I deserve."

⊙◦◦◦◦⊙

HAD she really thought Evan didn't scream Dom? She had thought that? Surely whenever she thought that, she must have been half out of her mind. To look at him now, no one would ever think him anything other than a Dom. He practically exuded it. She almost swore she felt it. And had she just agreed she wanted him to spank her?

Had she?

She was definitely not in her right mind. Though sitting on the couch not more than five steps in front of her, Evan waited, looking secure as if he knew with one hundred percent certainty there was only one way this thing was ending, and that was with her over his lap, her offered ass in the air for him to spank.

Fuck, she was going to do this.

She glanced over her shoulder to make sure the door to his cabin was closed and locked. It was. She took a deep breath and turned her attention back to Evan.

"Yes," he said, obviously seeing where she'd looked and guessing why. "The door is both closed and locked. This is a private matter between us and no one else has a right to know anything about it."

It was that last sentence that had her finally move her feet. Telling herself not to think about it above what was

99

necessary, she undid her jeans, pushed them down over her hips, and stopped for a second to catch her breath.

"How long has it been, Kelly?" Evan asked.

It didn't surprise her Evan knew exactly what she'd been thinking. She didn't hesitate before answering him honestly. "So long I can't even remember. Probably my first Dom."

He looked surprised at that, but didn't offer to forego his plan. Not that she expected or wanted him to.

With the truth of that fact echoing in her mind, she hooked her thumbs under the waistband of her underwear and pushed them down to join her pants on the floor. After that, it was only a few steps until she was in a position to drape herself over his lap.

Though it had been so long she couldn't remember the last time someone spanked her, her body remembered. In fact it shocked her how quickly she found herself settling her body in a way to both grant him access to her backside and to make everything as comfortable as possible for her.

"Very nice," Evan said. "Someone trained you well. Did you serve as a submissive before discovering you were a Domme?"

"Something like that," she said, not wanting to get into the whole switch thing while she was half naked and across his lap.

"Mmm," he hummed, running a hand over her ass. "I think you have the most spankable ass I've ever seen." He rained several light slaps across both cheeks. "Also, while I'm disciplining you, you will call me Sir."

She bit the inside of her cheek to keep any smartass replies inside her mouth where they belonged. As much as she might want to tell him to go fuck himself, she knew he was right. For this period of time she had given him control and calling him Sir would serve as a reminder.

"Do you understand?" he asked, and it didn't escape her attention that he waited before asking the question. *Because he knew she had to work it out before she would agree with him.*

She really didn't know how she ever saw him as anything other than a hardcore Dom. "Yes, Sir," she replied. With those two simple words, her body relaxed into a state of calm she wouldn't have expected to experience while naked and waiting over someone's knee for a spanking. Evan felt it as well, she was certain. No sooner had the tension left her body, than he whispered, "Good girl," and lightly swept his hand down her back. She swallowed a groan. She was not a submissive in Evan's eyes and she didn't want him to see her as anything other than Mistress K. No matter how incredible and right his hands felt on her or how warm her insides went at his praise.

Above her, Evan sighed, almost as if he could hear her thoughts. Then the first slap of his hand landed on her backside. At first they were light and sporadic, landing everywhere across the expanse of her ass. He was methodical, ensuring he didn't miss a spot. So gradual it took her longer than it should to notice the slaps became more focused and a lot harder.

The two of them had went back and forth over the years, teasing about the other's spanking abilities. He would crack some remark about how she hit like a girl and she'd come back with a well placed retort about how he had to spank because he'd never progressed beyond that point. After today, she would have to take back everything she'd ever said in relation to the way he spanked because, holy shit, did he know how. She already dreaded each smack of his hands and if she was right, he hadn't even started the real spanking yet.

"Okay," he said. "I think that's got you nice and warmed up. Are you ready for me to start now?"

Fucking hell. Even though she'd guessed correctly, it still came as somewhat of a shock that her butt was as sore as it was and he was only getting started.

"Kelly?"

"Yes, Sir," she replied. "I'm ready."

"Ask me properly."

She ground her teeth together. When he didn't budge, she squirmed, making sure she hit his erection as she did so.

He stilled her by placing his hand firmly on the small of her back. "Touch my dick one more time and you'll find it buried in your ass. Do I make myself clear?"

She froze at once. Not because of his words, although they were enough to fill her with an unexpected arousal. No. It was his tone. The unyielding and uncompromising tone that somehow made her insides quiver at the realization that she was indeed a switch. Even more as she realized Evan was one of the few Doms with the ability to bring out her long hidden away submissive self.

"Yes, Sir," she said. "I understand."

"Good," he said, using the same tone as before and

sending her insides to quiver once more. "Now I believe I'd also given you a command."

She didn't even hesitate. "Please, Sir. Spank me for my behavior toward you the last time we were together."

"See now how easy that was?"

Chapter Twelve

Evan probably should have kept that last comment to himself. Since the second she first realized his intention to spank her, not a single step had been easy for Kelly. Yet, she'd surprised him, and quite possibly herself, with the fact that she was naked from the waist down, and bent over his lap.

Spanking her wasn't even on the top of his list of things he wanted to do. Hell, with a half-naked Kelly draped over him, he could easily think of a dozen things that would be more fun. Spanking, or more to the point, causing any sort of pain had never been anything he looked forward to as a Dom. However, he'd lived this lifestyle long enough to know he'd spoken the truth when he told her they both needed this before they could move on.

With her ready and in position, he spanked her. He didn't go easy on her. There was no reason he should. She hadn't gone easy on him the day after the wedding, had she?

He spanked her until her ass was a bright red and his hand hurt. He spanked her until he saw tears rolling down her cheeks and she'd stopped trying to avoid his hand and accepted it as a just consequence of her actions.

When he brought his hand down for the last time, he told her they were finished. He wanted nothing more than to pull her tight to his chest and hold her. But, not knowing if she'd welcome anything of the sort, he hesitated for a second and simply stroked her back.

She must have taken his hesitation for something else because she sat up and threw her arms around his neck. "I'm so sorry I said those awful things to you."

"Shh," he shushed, putting his arms around her. "It's over. It's done with."

"Hold me," she pleaded. "Don't let me go yet."

His heart broke a little at her assumption that he would do differently. "I wouldn't dream of letting you go right now." He stroked her hair. "I'll hold you for as long as *I* need to hold you and I guarantee it'll be longer than you need."

She chuckled at that, which was why he said it.

He wasn't sure how long they stayed like that, her in his lap, both of them holding on to the other as if by letting go they would loose something precious. He'd already decided he wasn't going to pull away first. Whatever she needed and however long she needed it, she could have.

What he wasn't expecting was for her to turn her head slightly and whisper, "Take me."

"Kelly," he said, not sure it would be in either of their best interest to do anything further tonight.

"Please," she asked again. "I need... I need… you."

He wasn't sure he could be what she needed, and that killed him. He'd never gone from spanking someone to taking them to bed. Not a punishment type spanking. Sure, he typically got hard, but usually he'd ignore it and it'd go away. Occasionally, he'd have the submissive take him in her mouth. Never had any of them asked him to take her to bed.

No one except Kelly.

She pulled back and caught his gaze. "If you don't want me, tell me. But I thought… I thought you did and I need…"

He didn't let her finish. One, because he gathered she didn't know how to end what she was trying to say and two, because if she needed him, he would do whatever he could for her. If she needed the comfort of his body or the pleasure he could bring, it was hers.

"Stop," he barely got out before claiming her lips in a kiss to show he'd take her wherever and however she needed.

She tilted her head to give him greater access to her mouth and allowing him to deepen the kiss as he wanted. He slipped his hands under her shirt, basically a tee-shirt. All he had to do was draw her arms above her head and pull it off. Without a word, he unhooked her bra and gently slipped it off her as well.

God, she was even more beautiful than he remembered. Reverently, he trailed a finger down her neck, across her collarbone, and down her arm. He loved watching the goosebumps pop up along her skin and how she sucked in a breath at his touch.

"I'm yours," he told her. "For tonight, I'll be anything you need." Anything beyond tonight they would have to talk about. He still wasn't sure what made her lie the morning after the wedding. Wasn't sure what, if anything, she wanted in a relationship from him. But tonight, he could be whatever she needed.

Naked, she pulled back and gave him a sultry smile. A tentative sultry smile, but it was there, and it was all her. And something hit him in that moment, but it wasn't the time or place to discuss it, so he put it aside to talk about later.

Still holding her in his arms, he walked her backward to the bed until she bumped against it, and he pushed her down on her back. She didn't like being on top. Not that she had said it the last time they were together, but he could tell it wasn't her favorite.

Of course, that fit in just fine with what he was going to do because tonight, she wasn't Mistress K; she wasn't a Top, or a Domme. Tonight, she was his submissive, and he'd take her any way he wanted.

"You'll let me do anything I want to you tonight, won't you?" he asked, looking down at her, letting her feel how he'd pinned her to the bed.

"Yes, Sir," she whispered.

With those two softly spoken words, she'd handed him his favorite fantasy on a fucking silver platter. Kelly was his. At least for tonight. He might not let her sleep at all.

"Do you have any idea about all the things I want to do to you?" he asked.

"No, Sir."

He cupped her breast and ran his thumb over her nipple. "Would you like to find out?"

She moaned, but that wasn't good enough for him.

"Words, Kelly. Give me your words if you want to find out."

"It doesn't matter, Sir, what your plans are for me. I want you to take me however you want."

The words she spoke were so unlike anything he imagined coming out of her mouth. He lifted her chin to look into her eyes. "Are you telling me the truth, or saying what you think I want to hear?"

"The truth, Sir."

He sensed no falsehood in her expression. Maybe she didn't think the spanking was enough of a punishment, but then why had she almost begged him to take her? "What am I missing, Kelly? Talk to me."

Her gaze drifted away from his, and he knew he'd struck on something. She took a deep breath, and he feared she would remain silent. He'd never before wanted to be able to force someone to talk to him so badly, but force wasn't what she needed at the moment, so he waited.

It didn't take nearly as long as he thought, but her words were not anything like he'd expected. "I'm not a Domme. I'm a switch. It's been a long time since I've submitted to anyone. Much less for anything resembling a punishment spanking..." She paused, and he almost missed how her cheeks flushed as she spoke because he was still trying to work through her first two sentences. She was a *switch*? What the fuck?

He told himself to think about it later, because as unreal as it seemed, she was trying to tell him something she thought more important.

"I can't believe I'm going to tell you this but," she closed her eyes and continued, "I need you to punish me more."

Evan opened his mouth but nothing came out, which was just as well since she had more to say.

"Please, Sir." She opened her eyes. "I need you to fuck my ass."

He wasn't sure what to say or do. It was without question the oddest position he'd ever been in as a Dom. Sitting back on his knees, he brought her with him so they were both sitting on top of the bed.

"Look at me, Kelly," he said, taking her hand. When her eyes met his, he continued, "You don't need to feel as if you should offer yourself to me like that. Believe it or not, the idea to spank you didn't enter my mind until a few minutes before I brought it up. It's not as if I had a whole discipline scene planned. But we do have things to talk about: what exactly happened the morning after the wedding, how long you've been a switch, and most importantly, how to ensure we keep your sister safe."

She didn't agree with him right away and he hoped she didn't repeat her request. Turning down the offer of her ass the first time took a strength he didn't know he possessed. He doubted he could find it in him to do it a second time.

"Don't get me wrong," he said when it became obvious she wasn't going to talk. "I'd love to have your ass and, if it's something you'd like to explore together at another time, I'll be more than happy to oblige, but not like this."

She dipped her head and in doing so, several strands of her hair passed through a sliver of sunlight. He'd always thought her hair was glorious, but the way it looked in the sun, and the colors reflected? He fisted his hands so he wouldn't be tempted to touch.

"I've only had one relationship where I was a submissive." Though she spoke softly, he had no trouble hearing. "It was my first experience with a power exchange and I embraced it. My Dom always said spanking me made him hard and since it was my ass that made him that way, my ass would have to take care of it. I suppose only having had that experience, I assumed everyone did it that way." She laughed, startling him, but making him smile as well because her laugh had been so *real*.

"What?" he asked. "What's so funny?"

"It's just, I've been in the lifestyle how long? And one of things I've always drilled into everyone's head is there's not one true way and here I am thinking there's only one way to go about a spanking?" She shook her head. "How could I be so clueless?"

"Our past has a tendency to color our future and present more than we think." Having said that, he had an almost desperate need to know something else about her. "Out of curiosity, have you ever had anal sex that wasn't part of a punishment?"

"No. Never," she said. "Not that it matters, I can't imagine *that* ever feeling good."

He chuckled, and pulled her close to him, drawing them

both back down on the bed once more. "You have no idea what you just did, do you?"

"No. What did I do?"

He gave her a quick kiss and whispered in her ear. "You just made it a goal of mine to make you come during anal sex."

She cocked an eyebrow at him. "You and what army?"

"Are you saying you doubt I can do it?" He shifted them a bit, so the bedcovers rubbed against her ass.

"I would never tell the man who just spanked me as soundly as you did that I doubted his sex skills. I'm simply bringing up that *if* it were to happen it would take a hell of a lot of work."

"You realize nothing you just said will deter me?" He looked at her markedly but she didn't respond. "In fact, hearing you talk about it like that only makes me want to prove you wrong even more."

Chapter Thirteen

Though she left Evan's bed with a sore ass, Kelly had to admit she'd never left a scene in which she submitted feeling so good overall. It was a thought she carried with her that night and into early the next day while meeting a handful of other staff members.

Even now as everyone finished breakfast, and she watched Evan talk with Orson, she wasn't sure the day before had been real. Had he really spanked her and turned down her offer of anal sex?

And he had promised to make her come during anal sex?

Right. Like that would ever happen.

Not only that, but she never talked to anyone about her experience as a submissive. Never. Yet, she'd told Evan an earful. She wasn't sure why she kept that part of her life private other than she'd been known as a Domme for so long. Even with it being widely accepted that the best Tops also had experience as a bottom.

Why didn't she want people to know she, too, had that perspective?

Because you're afraid if you tell them they won't respect you as a Domme.

And that was the heart of it. All those Tops who had experience as a bottom that people thought were so great? They were all men. No one questioned a man. Although to be fair, no one had ever asked her if she had experience outside of being a Domme. It was only her fear or anticipation of such a reaction making her keep that part of her past private.

"What are you thinking about so hard over here all alone?" Kiara asked, sneaking up on her and catching her off guard. Kelly didn't react fast enough and Kiara saw exactly what, or rather whom, she was looking at. "Now he's a hottie. He can saddle me up for a ride any day."

"Are you talking about Orson or the guy he's talking with?"

"Don't think for a second I don't recognize the alpha male hotness that is Orson Kent. Hell, I'd saddle myself without waiting for him to do it if I had the slightest inkling he wanted to ride. Unfortunately, all I've heard since we arrived is how he never dates or plays with anyone with ties to the ranch."

Kelly thought that was interesting because she'd been at the ranch just as long as her sister and she hadn't heard the first thing about Orson's personal life.

"No," Kiara said, interrupting her thoughts. "I'm talking about the cowboy next to him."

"Evan?" Kelly asked, not expecting the sharp stab of jealousy that twisted in her gut.

"You know him?""

Kelly would give up almost anything to make her sister happy but she drew the line at Evan. "I suggest you look elsewhere for entertainment. Orson assigned Evan as the primary point of contact for your security."

"Oh, *that's* him." Kiara shrugged. "I wasn't able to meet him last night. He showed up late for dinner."

"That's because he was with me," Kelly stated as calmly as possible. "Number two reason you should look elsewhere. He's mine." Not technically, but she wasn't about to confess that to her sister. Especially with the way her twin looked at him as if he was a tasty treat waiting for her to devour. Kiara had told Kelly that she identified as a submissive, but didn't have much experience in the lifestyle. Which made Kelly wonder if she'd submitted to Randy? Although if her sister's main exposure to BDSM had been with that bastard, she found it hard to believe Kiara would elect to work at the ranch.

"Damn girl." Kiara took a step back and looked her up and down. Kelly was glad to see her sister's jovial side, but she couldn't say she was all that thrilled with the way Kiara kept on and on about Evan. "Okay, I get it. Hands off. I've never heard you utter such things about a man before. Must be serious."

"We knew each other in Wilmington but nothing really happened until I went back for the wedding."

"And he just *happened* to show up here?"

Hearing it again, this time coming from Kiara's mouth and not hers, once more brought up how crazy the entire situation was. "He and Orson were college roommates."

"Can you imagine those two in college?" Kiara asked and Kelly knew she had to get away before the conversation went further south than she wanted.

"I can actually," she told her sister, then gave her an eyebrow wiggle and a wave before turning to go outside.

She hadn't gone two feet before she noticed his presence.

"Was that your sister?" Evan asked.

"Yes." Kelly glanced over her shoulder, and damn he looked good. "I told her we were together last night, and that's why you were late to dinner."

"Really?" He'd caught up and walked by her side now, a self-satisfied grin at her words. "I'd hate to be a point of contention between the two of you."

"Trust me, you're not," she shot back. "I told her you were mine."

He stopped walking. "You did?"

"Yes, I did. Besides, you were her second choice. Orson caught her eye first but apparently he's so off limits she didn't even bother asking."

"Did you?" he questioned her as they began walking again.

"Did I what?"

"Did you ask if Orson was available?"

"Are you kidding me? When the hell do you think I had a moment to even think about Orson?" Evan was out of his mind. That explained his ridiculous question.

"Sorry. I went all caveman on you with no warning."

"Don't do it again."

"The thing is this." His smile was all mischief and merriment. "Since you told your sister I'm off limits, I'm left with a bit of a problem."

They were about midway to the cabins that would hold the training sessions. It was nearly time for the first session to begin and people were strolling along the grassy area in front of the rustic building or standing around and talking.

"How does that create a problem you?" Kelly asked.

"The training we have after lunch will be interspersed with demos. Orson asked me to lead one, and I'd thought to ask Kiara to do it with me. Since we'll be working close together and all that." He sighed. "I hesitate to ask her now that I know the two of you have had words about me."

Hell, fucking no. Kelly wasn't about to watch Evan demo anything with another woman. And she definitely wasn't going to watch him do those things with her sister.

"I can be your sub for the demo." At his raised eyebrow she added, "I remember telling you last night I was a switch." It hurt that after all they'd been through and done together, she wasn't his first choice.

The look of shock on his face told her maybe she'd read the situation incorrectly.

"You would do the demo with me?" he asked. "You were my first choice, obviously, but I wasn't sure how active a role you wanted with the hands-on stuff and then since most everyone knows you as a Domme, I didn't think you'd want to be in a submissive role."

She held her hand up. "I get it. Really, I do. How about this? While we're at the ranch, we're exclusive." She didn't know who, if anyone, he was playing with in Delaware and she could handle that. But not here. Here she couldn't stand the thought of seeing him with another woman.

"I don't have any issue at all with that," Evan said. "But don't you think you should ask what the demo is first?"

"Why? What's the demo?"

That damn smile was back on his face as he answered. "Anal." He held both of his hands up. "Don't look at me like that. I'm not the one who came up with the topics. Orson gave it to me this morning. It had nothing to do with what we discussed last night."

Kelly was the one who'd insisted she hadn't had time to think about Orson. Didn't the same apply to Evan? "I believe you."

"Good," he said, and she was glad his jovial voice was back, along with his easy grin. "It's a pain in the ass when a Dom starts a scene with the sub thinking he's a liar."

KELLY HAD TAKEN part in so many demonstrations throughout the years she hadn't thought twice about agreeing to do one with Evan. The realization that for this demo she would be the submissive partner, along with all the differences that entailed, didn't hit her until Evan told her to take all her clothes off.

"Are you kidding me?" she asked him when he came by the room she was getting ready in. "You want me to walk out there naked?"

"Frankly, I find you pretty damn hot in those thigh-high

boots and the leather corset but I don't think they're acceptable for this scene."

And that's when it hit her. Because she was the submissive.

Holy fuck what had she gotten herself into? What the ever loving hell had she been thinking?

Evan frowned. "I'm certain I told you I needed a submissive."

"You did." Kelly felt like an idiot. "I just didn't put the two together and well…" There was nothing else to add.

"Look at it from the positive angle," Evan said.

"I'm the submissive in an anal scene. What could be the positive angle?"

"For one, it's focusing on sensual elements and not discipline." He took a step back and appeared to be thinking something over. "You know, now that I think about it, you are the perfect person for this scene."

She snorted and wondered if there was a LIES DOMS TELL book she could add that one in. "Why is that?"

"Want to make a bet?"

She raised an eyebrow. Was he serious?

He took a step closer to her and the already small room seemed to get even smaller. It was almost as if Evan had grown two feet overnight or something the way he loomed over her. "Let's make it interesting. You're so certain you'll hate anything anal? I'm going to bet I can make you come from anal during the demo."

"I'm not sure I feel comfortable making a bet on something like that. It doesn't seem right."

"Why? Because you think you might lose?" He was so close now, she smelled the mint of the toothpaste he used. "Would it be so bad if you lost Kelly? We didn't even discuss what the wager would be."

"Maybe because it doesn't matter to me one way or the other what the wager is." She spoke the words, but she didn't believe them.

"Think about it," his voice had taken on a seductive quality she didn't remember hearing him use before. How was that possible? He reached up and stroked her forehead. "If you lose, it's because I gave you an orgasm? Is that really losing?"

He made sense, and really, it was a complete lose/lose situation for him. She'd already told him she'd never climaxed from anal, and it was unlikely he would be the Dom to end that streak. Besides, she hadn't had anything resembling anal sex for at least six years. There was no way on planet earth she'd have an orgasm tonight. Not the way he was planning to have it happen, anyway.

Though she felt a little bad that he wouldn't be able to make her come in a roomful of new peers. He'd probably feel a little embarrassed, but was that really her fault? He was the one pulling the *I can make you come with my mad Dom skills* routine, not her.

"Let's say I hypothetically take you up on this offer," she said. "What do you see the wager being?"

"If I can't make you come, I'll submit to you during a demo of your choice, *and* I'll let you Top me during a private scene."

"Why would you do that?" she asked. "I told you I don't fuck the men I Top."

"Number one, we've already fucked, so I don't see what that has to do with anything. Number two, even if you don't fuck them, I'm sure you get them off some other way. Frankly, that's just a lost orgasm for you. And three, maybe I'm into exploring my sexuality a bit."

Kelly didn't know how to reply to anything he'd just said or even where to start to unravel it all. She latched on to the last thing he'd said. "Do you think you're a switch?"

He shrugged like it was nothing. "I don't know. I've never given it much thought. But I know when I see you with a male submissive, I feel jealous. And in the hotel room when you told me to keep my hands still and you took me in your mouth, I experienced the best blow job I'd ever had. Maybe I want to explore that a little more."

It made sense when he laid it all out there like that. Not to mention, it sounded like a pretty good deal for her as well. She would be able to Top him twice. Once in public and once in private. If he thought he'd liked the way she gave him a blow job, she was willing to bet she had another trick or two up her sleeve he'd enjoy.

"Okay, you're on," she said.

He laughed. "We haven't even discussed what happens if I make you come."

It was such an improbability she didn't see the point in discussing it, but she supposed she should, to make it look fair.

"Okay then," she said. "What do you think would be appropriate if you're able to make me come?"

"I'm not sure what you know about the demo today."

"Nothing other than what you told me. Sensual, not punishment. Anal, of course."

Evan nodded. "Orson asked me to only use toys and fingers."

She couldn't resist dropping her gaze to his crotch which already sported the beginning of an erection. "So you're not allowed...?"

"My dick stays in my pants for the entire scene." He leveled his gaze at her. "At least the public part."

The lightbulb clicked on in her head. "As opposed to the private part?"

"Yes, if I can make you come in public during the demo without my cock in your ass, then you will also allow me the chance to make you come in private with it in your ass."

"Seems fair," she said, but suddenly she didn't know if his failure was as certain as she'd thought seconds before.

TEN MINUTES LATER, naked and bound over a smooth spanking bench, in front of people she didn't know all that well, Kelly's confidence in her ability rapidly regained strength. Kiara was at a meeting with the rest of the medical staff, and with Kelly and Evan both involved with the demo, Orson had also gone with her.

Evan was out of his mind if he thought there was even a remote possibility of her reaching orgasm in their current situation. He finished strapping her ankle and asked if everything felt okay. She assured him it did.

He turned and addressed those in the room, explaining what the demo was, and briefly that while the two of them knew each other, they had never played in public before. He never once mentioned whether she was a submissive or a switch, and though they hadn't discussed it, she was glad he didn't feel the need to explain every detail of their relationship.

Nor did he mention the bet. Not that she expected he would.

She had almost gotten to the point of tuning him out entirely when he got her attention with a question he asked those present.

"How many females here have ever had an orgasm from anal sex?"

No one seemed shocked with the relatively few positive replies.

"That seems to be a common problem," he continued. "So, this afternoon we're going to look at ways to remedy that."

He turned toward her. She saw the blindfold in his hand, and at once she knew he'd won.

"I should have lied when you asked me how any orgasms I'd had from anal sex," she said in an angry whisper.

"No," he replied just as softly, leaning in close. "You should have asked me how many of my anal sex partners have never orgasmed." He tied the blindfold around her head, nibbled her earlobe, and whispered. "The answer is none."

Chapter Fourteen

Years ago, before the Partners Group had ever entertained building a private club, parties and meetings were typically held in the member's private residences. Evan remembered at one party held at Kelly's house, he'd ended up pulling door duty because he called Kelly a she-devil numerous times.

He couldn't remember why he'd settled on that name instead of the other things he could have called her. More than likely it was another jab at her hair. However, he'd never seen her look more like she might actually sprout horns and use a pitchfork to toss him in a lake of fire than she did at that moment. And that was with a blindfold on.

Fortunately for him, the audience couldn't see her face the way he had her positioned. They knew who she was, at least they did if they'd been in the room when she walked in. But he'd picked up on her sensitivity surrounding anal sex and he'd wanted to shield her privacy as much as possible during the demo. Especially since he had all intentions of ensuring she had an orgasm.

Hoping his touch would cool her ire a bit and assuming it had a better chance of working with the blindfold on, he lightly brushed his thumbs across her forehead. "Relax, Kelly," he said. "Take deep breaths and let all the tension drain from your body."

"It'll take more than deep breaths to keep me from tying your balls into a knot when you release my hands."

Some of those gathered gasped, and a few snorted.

"Shit," Kelly said. "Everyone heard that, didn't they?"

That made the entire audience laugh. Evan decided there was nothing else to do other than to roll with it.

"Like I said," he told them, hoping he could carry off the not-so-quite-real smile he wore. "Kelly and I have known each other for years, but this is our first time playing together." He tapped her ass. "One more outburst like that and we'll make this an anal discipline session."

She wisely kept silent.

He addressed the audience again. "I've been asked to limit this demo to my fingers and toys. I think that's a good place to start if you or your partner are new to anal or have had a less than enjoyable prior experience. I've also found a submissive is more likely to relax if they know from the start the session won't end with a cock up their ass."

While talking, he'd kept his hands on Kelly. In his experience, any type of anal play was typically more enjoyable for a sub when they'd already had at least one orgasm. It was a given in his mind that at this point he had less than a snowball's chance in hell of Kelly having an orgasm soon. All he hoped for was to get her as relaxed as possible.

Orson had ensured that those working at the ranch on weekends all had significant lifestyle experience. The training and demos were more to get everyone started on an equal footing. As a result, all of those watching him at the moment knew his primary focus was Kelly and not them.

Since she wasn't as relaxed as he liked, when he finished addressing the group, he turned his attention to her entirely. He didn't care what was next on the schedule or when it was due to start. He would do everything in his power to bring Kelly pleasure. Which meant the first thing he had to do was get her to calm down.

And while it was true they'd never played in public before, they had been intimate, and he knew a thing or two about her body. He slipped noise cancelling headphones over her ears. Then, he went about using all the knowledge he'd gained to first, calm her body and, once he felt the tension leave her muscles, to transition to sensual touches.

She fought him to start, but the body didn't always follow orders given by the brain and before too long, her body hummed. When he finally had her at the place he wanted, he spoke to the audience in hushed tones.

He went over basics they all knew: anatomy, the differences between the sexes, and the importance of lube. Again, he kept his hands on her, stroking, and teasing. He detailed to the group the steps he would take and his outline of bringing Kelly to orgasm, explaining he would not talk them through the steps as he preformed them because he would focus only on the submissive in his care.

It was another thing he loved about being a Dom. Using everything he possessed to bring pleasure where there was none before. Even though she couldn't hear him, he whispered to her as he went through the plan he'd created his mind. In low tones no one would hear, he thanked her for her trust, told her how much she pleased him, how her body's responses turned him on.

He used his fingers first, drawing her arousal from her pussy to her ass and then adding more from the tube he brought. Every move he made was slow and methodical, and each one preformed with the sole intention of her orgasm.

Her breathing sped up as she grew closer and closer. He intensified nothing, watching for her to fight the path her body wanted, and he barely contained his shock when she instead whispered, "Green."

The temptation was strong to move faster, to fuck her with one of toys he'd brought, but thus far, she'd responded to slow. He'd be damned if he'd change his strategy now. "Stay with me, Kelly," he whispered, knowing she couldn't hear him. He spoke to her through his touch, telling her he understood her need and he would take her there. But on his timetable. In his own way.

She became malleable under his hands, and he used that to draw her sighs of pleasure out longer, to make her gasps of delight sharper, and her heart to race faster. He sensed her climax approaching, and he kept his touches slow, beckoning her release by increasing only how hard he touched her.

When she finally came, he watched as she welcomed it with her entire body. It was without a doubt the hottest thing he'd ever seen. The most telling thing, though, was the absolute silence surrounding them. No one in the audience made a sound. Evan wasn't even sure anyone dared to move.

He'd prepared a room earlier for aftercare, so he could tend to Kelly in private. But first he had to get her there. He slid the headphones off first and whispered he'd remove the blindfold next. He smiled at the way her eyes tentatively opened.

"How are you feeling?" he asked.

"Mmm," she hummed in reply. "That was incredible, Sir."

He wasn't sure which surprised him more, that she admitted readily how much she'd enjoyed it or that she'd called him 'Sir.' They both hit him square in the chest. He bent to unbind her, hoping the action would prevent her from seeing how strongly they both hit. "I'm so glad to hear you say that."

"So incredible I've decided I'm not going to tie your balls in a knot, Sir."

The faint laughter of those watching surrounded them.

He undid the last buckle, helped her up, and covered her in a blanket. "My balls thank you," he said, sweeping her into his arms and placing a soft kiss to her forehead.

⊙⊙⊙⊙⊙⊙

THOUGH SHE ENJOYED PROVIDING aftercare to the submissives she played with, Kelly remembered not caring

for it too much herself when she was with her first Dom.
Not that she had given it a lot of thought, after all, it had
been years since she submitted to anyone in a formal
scene.

Evan had cuddled with her for quite some time after he'd
spanked her, but she hadn't considered that to be aftercare.
Though at the moment, she couldn't remember why. It
had been nice, and she'd enjoyed being in his arms. Yet
again, when she'd agreed to do the demo with him, she
hadn't thought of the end of the scene nor had she
considered that he'd provide aftercare.

Evan, however, had been leap years ahead of her.

He'd brought her into a dimly lit room. Too small for a
bedroom and too large to be a closet, no doubt Orson had
given precise specifications for the building of this room. If
for no other reason than it was improbable an architect
would design such a room on their own.

There was no bed, but the space had been outfitted with a
comfortable lounger. Which is where he sat with her in his
lap, the warm blanket he'd taken from the other room still
wrapped around her. Someone had brought the clothes
she'd worn earlier. She supposed they should talk about the
scene or how she felt or even when he'd want to claim his
wager, but for the life of her she couldn't get her mouth to
open.

Evan chuckled.

"What?" she asked, finally finding her voice.

"You think too loud," he said.

"How is that even possible?" And why did everyone say
that to her?

"Damned if I know. You're the only person I know who does it."

She didn't know how to respond to that, so she didn't.

His arms tightened around her. "It wasn't an insult, and I didn't say it to start anything. I just wanted to point out that there's nothing wrong with thinking, but don't do it to the detriment of those around you."

"I don't know what you're talking about."

"Think all you want, but make sure you're talking to those you need to."

Did she do that? She supposed she did. "I guess I don't want to feel like a burden to anyone. It seems easier to work things out in my head."

He stroked her cheek, and she tried not to concentrate on how good it felt. "Your thoughts will never be a burden to those who care for you."

Does that include you? But she couldn't form the words. And then she didn't have to because he dropped his head and brushed his lips across hers.

It was a nice kiss, but she wanted more. She turned and straddled him, not caring the blanket fell from her body. So what? He'd seen her naked before.

"I don't think it's fair you didn't get to come during that demo." She ran her hands down his chest and stopped so they rested on his erection.

"The demo wasn't about me," he said through clenched teeth. Probably because she'd moved and now cupped him.

"But it should have been about you. You did all the work, I

only reaped the benefits." She squeezed, just a little. "Let me make it up to you." A delicate lick of his earlobe. "Please."

"Damn it, Kelly," he said. "There's not a man on this earth who can turn down an invitation like that."

"Then don't." She slipped her fingertips under his waistband.

"Not here." He pulled her hand away. "Not surrounded by peers and colleagues."

"Damn." That's right, they were on the other side of the door. "I have to be honest, I don't think I can sit through four hours of techniques, tips, and demos." She'd go mad. Partly because it would probably be a rehash of stuff she already knew and partly because she'd be horny as hell and that would not be fun.

"Me either."

"But we can't stay in this room for that long."

"Then it's a good thing there's a door, right behind me that leads outside."

They left as quietly as possible, not wanting to bring any attention to themselves. Not that anyone cared they'd left early. Evan told her he had mentioned to Orson they might leave after the demo and not stay for the rest of the sessions. Thank goodness for that.

She glanced over to where he walked by her side. Her mind still hadn't been able to grasp that Evan, the Evan she'd known for forever and a day, was the same man who gave her the most intense orgasm of her life just moments ago.

They made it to his secluded cabin within a matter of minutes. They didn't say much on the way but she acutely knew of every movement he made. What the hell was wrong with her when she lived in Wilmington? How was it she had been around Evan for years, talked with him, argued with him, and yet somehow had never *seen* him?

He stopped in front of the door and turned to look at her. "Do you want to pick up where we left off? We don't have to. It's up to you."

We don't have to have anal sex today, he was telling her, and while that was nice and sweet and everything, he had to be kidding. She meet his gaze. "I want you to take my ass. Take it and make me forget anyone's ever been there other than you."

He raised an eyebrow.

"Sir," she added. She had every intention of submitting to him for the evening, that didn't mean she would make it easy for him to dominate her.

He nodded. "Once we're inside, I want you to go to the bedroom and undress. I'll join you shortly."

"Yes, Sir," she said, because between his deep voice, the simple command, and memories of what he did to her body not that long ago, there was no other answer to give him.

Without another word, he opened the door to let her in first.

⋘⋙

Minutes later, she knelt on the rug in the cottage's

bedroom, anticipation building with every second he made her wait. It was both similar and not at all like the feeling she experienced as a Top when she made a sub wait for her. Though the differences were obvious, the sameness surprised her.

"Just when I think you can never look more beautiful, you prove me wrong." Evan's voice was smooth and seductive, his tone low and even, working together to sweep over her like a sensual caress. Never before had a voice been so tangible. "Stand up for me, Kelly."

She rose to her feet, disappointed to find he stood behind her, making it impossible for her to see him. This was another thing she was not used to in a scene. She'd been the one in charge for years. Not the one who obeyed. And yet, there was an indescribable flutter in her belly now that she was.

He moved to stand at her back, the nearness of him heating her skin. His hands cupped her shoulders and his lips brushed her ear. "Thank you for trusting me with this," he whispered. "Walk with me."

In that moment, she would have followed him anywhere, but he only took her as far as the bed. With a gentle hand, he pressed on her back.

"Lean over and made sure you're comfortable. Keep your legs spread." As he did in the demo, he kept his hands on her the entire time he talked. "You are magnificent. Every part of you."

His hands brushed over her backside. Teasing. Taunting. It was easier for him to do so this time as opposed to the demo. Mostly because then she tried so hard not to let him in her head, and this time she wanted him there.

By the time his hands made it between her legs, she was already wet and needy for him. He murmured a remark about how hard her responsiveness made him. Between his words and touch she hovered near the edge of her release sooner than she'd thought possible.

"No holding back," he said. "Not today. Today you come whenever you can because the more times you come, the more relaxed and ready you'll be for me."

With the next stroke of her clit her first orgasm hit.

"You're so sexy when you come," he said.

She glanced over her shoulder. "You think that even watching my backside?"

He gave her ass a playful slap. "I think that especially watching your backside."

It was impossible for her to argue back at that point because he had just dribbled lube between her butt cheeks. She tensed but only for a second and then made herself relax with thoughts of how intense her release had been at the demo.

"You're fucking perfect," Evan whispered above her as he slipped a finger inside her tight back hole. Though his fingers were larger than the toys he used previously, he had no trouble fitting them in.

"You are so damn perfect. I might never let you out of my bed."

He took his time fucking her with his fingers, but she found it wasn't enough to allow her to come a second time. "Please," she begged, knowing it was close but that she needed more than his fingers. "Please, Sir, fuck me."

"You think you're ready for me?" he asked, his voice much rougher than it had been moments before.

"I don't know. I just need…." her voice trailed off at the sound of a condom wrapper crinkling. Seconds later he was at her entrance, easing in. "Fuck, yes. Like that, Sir."

She took at deep breath as he pulled out and on his next thrust, he was completely inside her.

"Fucking hell," he cried out.

She was so full; she wasn't sure she could breathe. It didn't hurt; she was only full. Yet, he remained still; frozen inside her, like he was afraid to move.

"Please," she whispered and let out a moan when he slowly retreated.

"Did you know it's possible to hit your G-spot from here?"

She hadn't known that, but it was believable and she had no doubts he could. He moved in and out slowly a few times. Nice and easy. But she felt the need his hands couldn't hide, and she felt that need growing deep inside herself as well.

"I'm going to really fuck you now," he warned. "However, I won't come until you do."

She'd have loved to have teased him on that. To hold off her own pleasure, forcing him to hold off his. But his mastery of her body left her no way to do so. Especially when he hit a place deep inside and her resolve crumbled.

He tugged her hair, and she let her body take over. Her release hit ten times harder than it did at the demo. She was vaguely aware of a roar as he allowed himself to follow, but her eyelids grew heavy and refused to stay open.

"Shh," he whispered as she drifted off and cuddled into the warm body at her side. "Shh, just sleep and let me hold you."

⊙━⊙━⊙━⊙

A POUNDING on the door woke Evan up. It took him a second to realize where he was, and another to remember he wasn't alone. Beside him, Kelly stirred, but didn't wake. Evan eased out of bed, wanting to let her sleep, when the pounding came again. Only this time, a loud voice accompanied the beating of the door.

"Evan! I need you to let me in if you're in there." It sounded like a very upset Orson.

Evan looked at the clock while tugging his pants on. Just after nine o'clock at night. It was dark out, but hadn't been that way for long. Kelly sat up, and pushed the hair out of her eyes.

"What is it?" she asked, still half asleep.

"Orson, I think," Evan said. "I'll go see what he needs and take care of it all. You can go back to sleep."

She sat up higher and gave him a seductive smile. "Not without you. Hurry back."

Evan jogged to the door, hoping whatever crawled up Orson's ass could find a way back out in the next three minutes. He had a warm Kelly waiting for him in his bed and he wasn't about to leave her longer than necessary.

But as soon as he opened the door and saw Orson's expression, he knew there'd be no more warm bed and Kelly tonight.

"I heard you talking to someone inside," Orson said, his face filled with the oddest combination of grief and anger Evan had ever seen. "Please, God, tell me it was one of the twins."

Kelly appeared at Evan's side almost instantly, the bed sheet still wrapped around her. "It's me. Where's Kiara?"

"Kelly," Orson said. "Thank goodness."

"Where's Kiara?" she asked again, her voice an octave higher.

"They've taken her."

Chapter Fifteen

Kelly took a deep breath. One. It was all she allowed herself to have.

In.

Stay calm.

Out.

It's the only way.

It wasn't nearly enough, but it would have to do. At least for now.

"Tell me what the fuck happened," she said in the calmest voice she could manage. Which sounded pretty calm to her ears. The only thing exposing her true feelings were her trembling hands. She balled them into fists.

"I was with her at the medical team meeting and everything was fine," Orson said. "We ended around four thirty. Kiara told me she was going to her room to rest before dinner, said she had a headache. I walked her to her room, saw her safely inside, and told her to call for me when she was ready for dinner."

Dinner was at six thirty. It was now past nine, Orson needed to hurry. Only her years of experience in talking with witnesses kept her from unleashing on him. She could spare a few seconds.

Evan, however, had no such experience. "Dinner was almost three hours ago. What the fuck is going on?"

Kelly moved to stand in between the two men. "Let him finish, Evan. Orson, continue. Quickly, please."

Orson nodded, the grief in his eyes clearer than before. "At six-thirty when I hadn't heard from her, I sent her a text, but she didn't reply. I waited a few minutes and then I called. No answer." He shook his head. "I thought she was asleep, and I didn't want to wake her up. I didn't eat myself, just stood around talking and waiting for her to call me. At seven, I called her again. When I didn't get an answer, I made us both a plate and carried them to her room."

"Two hours ago," Evan said, his voice tinged in anger. "Quicker."

Orson nodded. "I knocked and told her she needed to get up. I said I had dinner for us and we could eat outside. There was still nothing. I went by Kelly's room to see if she'd seen her, but you weren't there and then I remembered I hadn't seen you at dinner either."

Kelly couldn't help but to cringe at that. *Because she and Evan had been too busy fucking to stop for dinner.* Beside her, Evan took a deep breath.

Orson continued, "It didn't cross my mind to call you. Since I wasn't sure where either you or your sister were, I used a master key to unlock her room. She wasn't there. I... I didn't want to touch anything."

"Did you call the police?" Evan asked.

"I don't think this area falls in a police district. Sheriff probably?" Kelly looked at Orson and he nodded. Even though she wanted to break down and rage in equal measure, she did neither. This wasn't time for emotions. Emotions could come later. She had to be smart and distance herself from the situation. "Even if we called someone, Kiara's an adult. She has every right to leave the ranch if she wants to."

"But we know that isn't what happened," Evan said.

"I need to see her room," Kelly said.

"I'll take you," Orson replied. "But you should probably get dressed first."

Kelly looked down. She'd forgotten she only had a sheet wrapped haphazardly around her. With a nod, she turned back to Evan's room. She refused to look at the large bed she'd recently vacated and under no circumstances would she think about what her and Evan were doing in that bed when her sister went missing.

With shaky hands, she forced herself to dress, telling herself she had to be strong and keep it together. Her only focus was to get Kiara back safely. She found her phone buried under a quilt on the floor and saw it was still in the silent mode she'd put it in before the demo. Wouldn't have done any good even if Orson had tried to call.

There were no notifications from Kiara.

She pocketed the phone and went back to the main room where both men waited. "I haven't received anything from Kiara. If she was going off somewhere on her own, she'd have let me know. My assumption is someone took her." She turned to Orson. "Which is what you said when Evan opened the door. 'They've taken her.' Those were your words. Not, 'She's missing' or 'We can't find her,' but, 'They've taken her.' Why those words?"

"I've talked to your sister quite a bit since she's arrived and I know her well enough to know she wouldn't walk away like that." Orson looked defensive for the first time. "It's the only other option."

Kelly took a step toward him. "Just how well have you gotten to know Kiara?"

"I don't like what you're insinuating," Orson said. "Why is it okay for you to assume someone took her and not for me to reach the same conclusion?"

"Because only someone who took her would know she hadn't tried to reach me."

Orson threw his hands up. "Why the hell would I kidnap Kiara? What purpose would it serve?"

"Why the hell is it almost nine-thirty and I'm only now hearing about this?" So much for keeping her emotions in check.

"Because you were too busy -"

"I suggest you not finish that sentence." Evan interrupted, stepping in front of Orson. "Let's all go over to Kiara's room and see if Kelly can find anything."

She should probably thank him for ending that

conversation before it got out of hand, and the best thing she could do at the moment would be to look over Kiara's room for any clues, but Kelly didn't say anything to Evan on the way to Kiara's room. It was wrong, so wrong, but part of her blamed him for being in bed all afternoon.

They had almost made it to the building that housed their rooms when an employee ran up to them.

"Mr. Kent," the guy called. He held something in his hand.

They stopped and waited.

"Yes," Orson said.

"We found this over by the field on the family-side." He held out Kiara's watch.

Kelly gasped and Orson's gaze latched on her. "It's hers?"

Kelly nodded. "I gave it to her when she graduated from nursing school." The employee dropped the watch into her outstretched hand and she clutched her fingers around the smooth, cool face. "She only takes it off to sleep and to shower. There's no way she'd leave it in a field somewhere. She wanted me to find it."

But why? She could have left anything to be found. Why the watch? She turned it over. Nothing looked strange or out of place. No visible scratches. Nothing broken. All that told her was that it had been taken off. Not forced.

She looked back to Orson. "You watched her enter her room?"

"Yes, and I heard the door lock."

Did anyone see you? Can you prove it? She kept those questions

143

to herself. "Are there security cameras in that field and are they operational?"

"Yes, and yes." Orson typed something on his phone. "Security's been looking through all the video feeds. I just sent them a text and told them to pull those."

"What I don't get is how did that Randy guy find out she was here?" Evan asked. "We are assuming it's him, right?"

No, she was not ready to make that assumption, but based on Evan's reaction when she'd questioned Orson earlier, she would admit nothing to the contrary. "He's the most likely suspect," she agreed.

"So how did he know she was here?" Evan asked. "I remember you told me you didn't see anyone follow your car on the way here."

"I don't know," she had to admit. But there was one thing she could do. "Let me go make a quick phone call before I see her room."

Without waiting for a response, she walked a short distance to a nearby bench, sat down, and selected a contact in her phone. So far she had played everything by the book. She hadn't called in any favors or used her position for personal use. However, Kiara was in trouble and that meant all bets were off. She'd move heaven and earth and storm the gates of hell by herself if needed. She would find Kiara.

"Hey," she said, when the man answered his phone on the first ring. "It's Kelly Bowman. I need you to look into something for me."

FIVE MINUTES LATER, she stood in Kiara's room,

committing as many details to memory as possible. She didn't want to touch anything if she didn't have to; she was only looking over things. Orson and Evan waited for her outside. She'd told them it wouldn't take her too long, it was such a little space, and her time would be better spent on other things.

"Okay," she said a few minutes later, walking outside. "I'm finished."

Evan walked to stand by her side. She wanted so badly to bury herself in his arms, but she couldn't. Not right now. Not yet.

"Let's go to my office," Orson said.

No one said anything until they'd all sat down at a small conference table in Orson's office. Evan took a seat beside her. He didn't touch her or tell her it would all turn out okay. He was simply there. Which was what she needed at the moment. Orson sat across from them.

"Did you see anything in her room?" Evan asked.

"Her phone was gone," Kelly said. "She has a case she carries it in that holds her ID, some cash, and a card or two. That was also gone. But her toiletries, clothes, everything else was in its place. Wherever she planned to go when she left, she didn't think she'd stay long."

"So the question becomes, why did she leave her room?" Evan mused. "Did she get a text or did someone knock on her door?"

"To say someone knocked on her door is to suggest either an inside job or a security breach," Orson said.

"Yes." Kelly spoke the one word and turned back to Evan.

"Either way, how did her watch end up in that field? Why would she even be out that way?" She flicked her gaze to Orson. "How close are we on the security camera footage?"

"I got a text two minutes ago. They're running it now."

"I was thinking about how Randy could know where she is," Evan said. "Is the phone she's using now the same one she had when she was with him? And if so, is it possible he placed a tracking device on it or somehow downloaded a program on it, showing her location?"

Kelly made notes on her phone. "I'm not sure, but I'll see if I can find that information somewhere."

He made a good point. With something to track Kiara, there would be no need to follow her. He'd always know where she was.

"The other piece to this puzzle," she said. "And I don't think we can brush it off as a mere coincidence, is the fact all this happened while the three of us were... busy." She cleared her throat. "Which again points to an inside job."

Orson leaned forward. "No one had any idea you and Evan would be 'busy' after the demo. So you can cross that one off the list."

Kelly refused to back down and leveled her gaze at him. "No one but his boss, who he told *before* the demo that the two of us might not attend the remaining sessions."

"Are you still thinking I had something to do with this?"

"Let me set you straight, Mr. Kent. Right now I'm investigating a potential kidnapping. That means, you're not on trial. It also means you're *guilty* until proven innocent. That's how things are done in my world, so for right now I need for you to drop the wounded bystander act. Got it?"

Her phone buzzed on the table in front of her. Without looking to see who it was, she answered ."Yes?" She stood up. "That was faster than I expected. Have you found anything?"

She remained silent as he talked, only asking if he was certain when he finished speaking. He assured her he was, and she thanked him before ending the call.

Silently, she put the phone back down on the table. Damn, that hadn't gone the way she thought it would. She closed her eyes and wondered which path to take next.

"Kelly?" Evan asked.

She looked at him. His eyes held worry, not only for Kiara but also for her.

"I called in a favor with a friend of mine," she said. "Randy hasn't left Dallas all day. There have been eyes on him nonstop since he left his house at eight-thirty this morning."

She looked straight at Orson, knowing she didn't have to speak what that meant.

There was a knock on the door.

"Come in," Orson called out, tearing his gaze away from hers.

Seconds later two men with cowboy hats clutched in their hands made their way into the office. With heads down and refusing to make eye contact with anyone at the table, they made their way to stand beside Orson.

"Why are you two here?" Orson asked. "Your orders were to call me when you finished reviewing the security footage, so we could all come and watch together."

These two were part of Orson's security team? They looked like scarecrows. Kelly hoped they only dealt with the cyber part of that team.

"That's the thing, Boss," Cowboy One said. "We went through all the cameras on the family field. They didn't record anything."

Kelly snapped her pencil in half. "What do you mean they didn't record anything?"

"Ms. Bowman," Orson started, but Kelly shut him down.

"Don't say a fucking word," she told Orson. To the men standing at his side, she asked, "Why didn't they record anything?"

Cowboy Two replied. "From what we could put together, someone disabled all the cameras with a view of that field after lunch. They were still down when we looked and they've only been working again for the last five minutes."

"Tell me again, Mr. Kent," Kelly said in the soft voice her submissives swore could make a grown man pee his pants. "How this could not possibly be an inside job?"

Chapter Sixteen

Evan didn't attempt to talk Kelly into taking a break or stopping to rest. He knew how he felt knowing what they were doing when someone got their hands on Kiara. He felt like ten kinds of shit and imagined it was even worse for Kelly.

He did everything he could to help her: he stayed by her side, ensured everyone followed her commands, got her coffee, and made phone calls. Unfortunately, she'd been right and local law enforcement wouldn't classify Kiara's disappearance as suspicious yet, especially with Randy having an airtight alibi.

Hearing that only made Kelly work harder and as a result, everyone around her did the same. It was now well after midnight and the three of them had taken over the administrative building. Orson was in an empty office interviewing employees. He said someone had to have seen or heard something and he'd shake it out of people if he had to. Kelly had agreed for him to conduct the interviews even though Evan knew she still regarded the ranch owner as a suspect.

Not that he could fault her. Not the way everything pointed to someone inside the ranch being involved. Plus, Orson had been the only person he'd told about not returning after the demo. The problem with Orson as a suspect was the man had no reason to kidnap Kiara.

Not that he could imagine anyone at the ranch wanting to harm the other Bowman twin. By all accounts, Kiara was the bubbly and personable one. It was his own siren most saw as detached and standoffish.

At the moment, Kelly was elbow deep with a man she'd nicknamed Cowboy One and security videos. She'd said one of the operational cameras might have caught a snippet of something important. It was worse than a long shot. It was the proverbial needle in a haystack, but he knew her well enough to know she had to be doing something and currently, those videos were the only things keeping her from going off the deep end.

Evan glanced at her coffee cup and was getting ready to put down the employee files he'd looked over twice already to get her more, when the office door opened.

"Excuse me," it was Kelly's Cowboy Two, with a man Evan didn't recognize and hadn't seen around the ranch. "Officer K?"

Kelly stopped the video she'd been watching and Evan hoped whatever Cowboy and the unknown man had to say was important because based on her expression when she looked up, if it wasn't whatever followed would not be pretty. "Yes?" she asked.

Cowboy Two jerked a thumb to the man at his side. "This is Jed. He owns the property that adjourns the ranch."

Evan looked at Jed again. Unlike every other male who'd been in contact with Kelly tonight, he didn't cower at the fiery redhead. He stood with a confidence and an air of power, but the wrinkles at the corners of his eyes spoke of a man who laughed often.

"Jedidiah Oakes, ma'am," Jed said to Kelly and sent a nod Evan's way.

"Listen, Jedidiah," Kelly said. "We're busy here. Unless you have -"

Jedidiah stopped her by lifting his hand. "This is not a social call."

Kelly stood straighter. "I didn't think it was considering the time."

"I apologize for the lateness of the hour. I'd just returned from town when my housekeeper told me about the trouble you had here this afternoon."

Kelly clearly was biting her tongue. She had a lot more patience than Evan did. If Jed had been talking to him, he'd tell him to spit it out or leave. Instead, he stood and moved to stand next to Kelly.

"I think the disappearance of Ms. Bowman's sister ranks higher than *trouble*," Evan said. "And the fact that you've been in town this long leads me to believe you were at a bar. Do you have some information to pass along or are you only looking for gossip?"

Jed regarded him cooly, neither confirming nor denying

the bar statement. "I worked this afternoon on my pasture that runs along the side of your east field."

"That's the field where they found her watch," Cowboy Two added.

"Around five I noticed a truck going down the edge of your property," Jed said. "I thought nothing of it, I'd seen the vehicle before and recognized it as belonging to one of your employees. I assumed whoever it was had maintenance work to take care of."

Evan's heart pounded harder. This could be a clue, but beside him, Kelly still looked skeptical.

"A likely assumption, Jedidiah," Kelly said. "Interesting you thought it worth a trip over here to tell us you saw a ranch employee doing maintenance."

"That's not why I made the trip, ma'am."

Kelly waited.

"It was because twenty minutes later, the same truck returned going back the way it came and a lot faster. In fact, it was going so fast, I decided to speak to Mr. Kent about it later." Jed's voice was still as calm as it'd been since the moment he walked in the door. However, Evan felt Kelly's body tense as his words sank in.

"That time fits perfectly with when we think someone took Kiara," she whispered.

Jed nodded. "As soon as I heard there was a woman missing, I remembered that truck, and I made it over here as quickly as possible. I only wish I'd heard of her disappearance sooner. Or that I'd come right away with my concerns about how fast that truck was going."

"The important thing is you came, and you did it as soon as you could." Kelly was trying to contain her excitement, but it was hard, Evan could tell.

"I also brought some footage my security camera caught," Jed added, with a nod toward Cowboy Two, who held up a thumb drive. "I checked when I returned home to ensure it captured the truck. Thought it might be useful when I had my chat with Mr. Kent. Now I'm hopeful it'll be more useful in another way."

"Thank you, Jedidiah," Kelly said.

"No thanks, necessary, ma'am." Jed tipped his hat. "Let me know if you need my help."

No one moved until the door closed behind him. As soon as it clicked, Kelly looked at Cowboy Two. "Give me that thumb drive and get Orson in here."

⊙━◌━◌━◌━⊙

"Do you recognize the truck?" Kelly asked Orson as they watched a white pickup race across the computer screen in the footage Jed's camera caught. The thumb drive contained only a clip of the security footage; it didn't show the first time the truck went along the property line, only the second. Since Jed had planned on using the footage to complain about the driver's speed, the reason he clipped it made sense, but Kelly wished she had both. Not that it mattered in the short term. Jed had more than likely caught the first appearance on camera and could produce the footage if there was ever a need. God, she hoped there wasn't a need.

"Yes. I know that truck," Orson said, and from the

expression worn by both men of his technical security team, Mitch and Conner, though she preferred Cowboy One and Two, they did as well. "It looks like Seth's truck."

"Who is Seth?" Kelly had met many people and she was usually good with names, but she didn't remember a Seth.

"You probably haven't had the chance to meet him," Orson said. "He's a stable hand. He works some weekends here, but typically he doesn't come around the kink players."

"Have you interviewed him yet?" she asked.

Orson shook his head. "No. I thought it would make sense to speak with those who interacted with her first."

Which is what she would have done had she been the one in charge of interviews.

"I have his file right here." Evan placed a file folder in her hands.

Kelly opened the folder and scanned the papers inside. Nothing popped out as strange. All she saw were normal details: address, phone number, interview notes. "This has his address listed as Miller Road. How far is that?"

"Boss," Mitch said, before Orson could answer. "Seth's been staying overnight at the stables. That bay mare is due to foal and doc said someone should be with her at all times in case she goes in to labor."

Orson pinched the bridge of his nose. "Right, she's the one we almost lost."

Mitch nodded.

Kelly tried not to let her brain get ahead of things, but if Seth was the guy they were looking for and he had to stay close because of a horse…

She couldn't think it. Wouldn't let herself think there was a possibility Kiara could still be at the ranch.

But she did anyway.

All five of them started talking at once. As the only law officer present, she needed to ensure everything ran as smoothly as possible and no one did anything to mess them up. They were close; she knew it. Now was not the time to get overexcited and screw up. They needed to slow down and plan.

She closed her eyes to help in removing herself from the situation. This was just another case. Telling herself that was the only way she'd be able to get through it.

She opened her eyes.

"Quiet," she said and the four men stopped talking. "Thank you. Now, the first thing we need to do is to make sure this information stays with us. As of right now, we have a jump on a suspect, but if he hears we're onto him, this could go south fast."

The prior excitement dissipated and the expressions around the room grew somber once more. They weren't finished yet. They still had a long way to go.

"Is there anyone else staying here overnight who normally doesn't or any other employee we could bring in at the same time we bring in Seth, so he doesn't get suspicious?" Kelly asked.

"We could bring in Mac and his boy," Mitch said. "Seth wouldn't think anything was up if you brought those two."

"The ranch foreman and his son, JD," Orson added, with a knowing nod in Kelly's direction. "I agree. I've seen JD and Seth together several times."

She got the hint. If she was looking for a second party, JD could be a potential suspect.

"Will anyone think it's odd for Orson to bring the three of them in with it being after midnight?" Evan asked.

Kelly shook her head. "I don't think so. If Seth's supposed to be looking after a mare, he should be awake anyway. And I'm sure the foreman's used to getting called for whatever reason at all times of the night. More than likely, his son's used to it as well."

"Makes sense to me," Evan said.

"Mitch," Kelly said. "Go by the stables and pick up Seth. Then the two of you go to get Mac and JD. Don't ask him questions pertaining to Kiara, but if he asks them, answer as best you can. Conner, as soon as they leave the barn, I want you and Evan to look through it for anything, and I mean anything, that looks relevant to Kiara."

"Should we be subtle and use flashlights, or go all out and turn on every light in the place?" Evan asked.

"How about somewhere between the two?" she replied, with a weak smile. "I'd hate to cause a mamma horse stress."

Evan only winked.

As everyone headed out of the room to move forward with

the agreed-upon plan, Evan stayed behind. He said nothing, but took her hand and gave it a gentle squeeze. She did the same to his. He placed a kiss on her forehead and then slipped into the night with Conner.

Chapter Seventeen

The stables were a complete bust and Evan hurried ahead of Conner feeling guilty because he had to return to Kelly empty-handed and anxious because he wanted to see if anything came of the interviews. He hoped to hell Kelly or Orson had uncovered some kind of information because if not, he feared Kiara's outlook was turning more and more bleak with each moment that went by.

He'd been so certain something would turn up at the stables he wasn't sure what to do about the sense of failure that came over him. He was so wrapped up in self-deprecation, he almost missed hearing the heated whispers coming from two men just ahead, but he didn't recognize either voice.

Evan held out his hand to stop Conner and made a shush movement with his finger. Conner nodded, apparently also hearing the whispers. They stepped off the path to hide as much as possible. Looking around, Evan tried to place where he was at the ranch, and suddenly realized that the whispers were coming from the drive leading to the foreman's house.

There was no way that was a coincidence.

"I'm telling you, man, they have no fucking clue. If they thought for a second you were involved, they would have dropped everything, said, 'Screw protocol, we're taking this mother down now.' They let you go, bro. Chill."

"Yeah, easy for you to say, she wasn't in your vehicle. They could run fingerprints and do that DNA shit and know this crap involved me."

"Calm the fuck down. That would only prove your *truck* was involved, not you, and yes your prints would be on it, it's your truck. All you have to say is you loaned it to a friend, or it got stolen."

Evan was tempted to get his phone out to record the conversation or to send Kelly a text, but he feared the light of his cell would catch the attention of one of the guys arguing.

"Fine, but I still think we should move her."

"Seriously, what the fuck is your problem? We're leaving her right where she is. Stick to the plan. Tomorrow, we'll be able to get in contact with the man who wants her back so bad and we'll take him to her. If we move her again, we risk having her get away, like she almost did last time. And no, we will not go to her now, because you'll end up fucking her and then I'll have to kill you. Got it?"

"Got it." Though Evan didn't think Seth liked it very much.

"Good. Now I'm going to bed, before the old man comes

looking for me, and I suggest you do the same. We leave that bitch right where she is. If I find out you saw her without me, it won't be good."

"Fuck off. I'm not going anywhere tonight except the stable."

Evan waited until the sound of footsteps from both men faded away and then an extra minute before daring to talk to Conner. "I don't believe for a minute Seth's going back to the stable."

"I don't either," Conner agreed.

"You know this land and the surrounding area better than I do. Can you do your best to follow him while I get the others together?"

They agreed to split up. Conner would tail Seth and text Evan if he moved. Evan returned to the path and ran as fast as he could to alert Kelly and get everyone in position to head out. He wanted them ready to move the second he heard from Conner. In his gut, he knew he didn't have much time.

Which meant Kiara might have even less.

Evan found Kelly and Orson arguing, of course.

"I want to find her as well, but unfortunately it doesn't matter what you think the man's son might have done," Orson said to her, crossing his arms. "We can't go storming into his house without a warrant."

Kelly didn't reply since she'd seen reason at that point. She ignored Orson and turned to him. "What did you find?"

"The stable is clean, but we overheard Seth and JD. They definitely have her somewhere and somewhere close. We think JD will stay put for the night, Conner's following Seth. We need to get ready to head out if he sends word Seth's on the move."

Kelly gathered her things while still talking with Orson and Mitch. "If you had to keep someone hidden near here but not on the ranch where would it be?"

Mitch spoke first. "Those caves up near where Old Man Tucker used to live."

"Where are they?" she asked.

"About four miles."

"On Jed Oakes's land," Orson added.

Kelly froze. "Jedidiah Oakes? The man who gave us the thumb drive?" She paused but only for a second. "Do you think he knows something or could they get to the caves without his knowledge? And why would he tip us off if he knew where she was?"

"Lots of people used to go explore the caves," Mitch said. "But that was when Jed's dad was alive. I don't know about now."

"Orson?" Evan asked, because the man had his lips pressed together like he was struggling not to say something.

"I didn't say anything earlier because I thought it'd sound petty and I didn't want to be like that after he dropped the video off." Orson ran a hand through his hair. "But not everyone around here was thrilled when I bought the ranch and announced my plans. Jed Oakes was one of those opposed."

"What are you saying?" Evan asked.

"He's saying if Jedidiah wanted to run Orson out of business, something like this would be a good start." Kelly turned to Orson. "And yes, it sounds petty." Before Orson could reply, she added, "But I've seen people do worse for less. So it can't be discounted."

Evan's phone buzzed with an incoming text. "Seth's on the move."

Kelly seamlessly took control. "Evan and Orson, you guys come with me. Mitch, you stay here." She grabbed a duffle bag. "Let's go get my sister."

◑◒◐◓◑◒◐

KELLY DROVE her car with Evan relaying Conner's directions in the passenger seat while Orson rode in the back. She'd have liked it better if they could have left Orson behind at the ranch, but since he was both Seth's employer and Jed's neighbor, it was better that he came along.

According to Orson, they had entered Jed's land by the entranceway farthest away from the ranch. Conner was quick to point out it was the entrance closest to the caves. Kelly couldn't help but wonder if he'd been in contact with Mitch, since his teammate had been quick to suggest the caves as well.

Conner suggested she turn off her headlights so as not to announce their arrival. It was a good suggestion, unfortunately it made driving horrendously slow. She could walk faster. It helped she felt Evan's impatience growing beside her.

After what seemed like forever, but in reality hadn't been over thirty minutes, they reached the spot Conner had parked. They all got out of the car to get an update.

"The caves are about half a mile further up this path," Conner said. "That's where Seth went in his truck. I got out of my car and walked up to where I could see him but remain hidden. Based on the way Seth's been cursing and fumbling around trying not to use a light, I get the impression Ms. Bowman isn't where he left her."

"What?" Kelly asked. "What do you mean?"

"He's been huffing and puffing and mumbling under his breath about this is why he told that asshole JD they had to come back tonight," Conner said. "I have to give him some credit, he's not a total idiot. I watched as he looked for any vehicle track marks. Far as I can tell, he didn't find any."

"He thinks she somehow got away herself?" Evan asked.

"It seems to make the most sense if there's no evidence of another vehicle." Conner thought for a second. "The other possibility would be someone coming by on a horse and the only person who could do that is Jed."

Kelly didn't like how the neighboring rancher's name kept getting brought up whenever they came upon some new detail about Kiara's disappearance. Once was acceptable. Twice was odd, but believable. Now it had reached the stage where she was thinking he was a more appropriate suspect than Orson.

"Conner," she said. "Can you go back to the ranch and wait by the foreman's driveway? I'd like someone to be there in case Seth gets in contact with JD. Mitch is in the office building, but I need to keep him there."

"Sure thing, Officer Bowman," Conner said. "If he comes out, what should I do?"

"Try to stall him. If you can't, follow him, but keep your distance like you did with Seth. I doubt he can get into much trouble, but I'd like eyes on him as much as possible."

What she didn't add was that it'd make more sense for Orson to be waiting outside of the foreman's home but that she couldn't send him because she still didn't trust the man.

"You don't think it'd be better for me to go back to the ranch and keep guard outside Mac's house?" Orson asked, as if her brain had split wide open and he could see inside and read what she was thinking.

"You actually would be my first choice," she told him, and it wasn't a total lie. "But I'd rather you be here in case Jed were to come by. I think he'd be more likely to listen to you as opposed to me or Evan."

He nodded, seeming to take her answer for the whole truth instead of the half truth it was. She would feel comfortable with either herself or Evan talking with Jed *if* she knew beyond a doubt she could trust Orson. Since she couldn't, not completely, she'd rather the ranch owner stay where she could see him.

With that settled, Conner took off, and they remained where they were, trying to decide what to do or even if they should do anything. Perhaps the best course of action would be to wait until either Seth made a move or they could determine where Kiara might be.

"Do you think if Kiara's still around this area that she can see us?" Evan asked.

"I don't know," Kelly answered. "I'd like to think so, but then again if she can see us, wouldn't Seth be able to as well? I don't know if I want him aware of our presence just yet."

The three of them were silent for a few minutes. Evan moved a bit closer to where they could barely make out the shape of Seth pacing. God, she hated this. Kelly's stomach was in knots. She couldn't help but feel as if she'd missed some key detail or important bit of information, and she hated that she couldn't decide if it was a good thing or a bad thing Kiara wasn't where the men who took her left her.

They needed a plan. It was imperative they try to be as prepared for anything as possible.

"He's reaching for his phone," Evan warned, eyes still glued to Seth.

Kelly turned to Orson. "Get ready to call Conner. I don't know who else Seth would contact other than JD." How long ago had Conner left? She didn't think he'd had enough time to make it back to the ranch and get into position. Damn it. She needed someone watching JD.

Her phone was in her back pocket. Should she call Mitch and have him wait by the foreman's house? Better to have two men there as opposed to none.

She grabbed her phone, but hadn't started to pull up Mitch's contact information when she heard a gun click.

. . .

IT TOOK her a handful of seconds before she realized the sound came from the right of Seth and not anywhere near her or the two men with her. Kelly looked up ahead to where the stable hand now stood with his hands in the air. A taller figure rose in the shadows beside him, too far away from any source of light for her to make out who it was.

But as soon as the figure spoke, she recognized Jed Oakes. "I'll give you three seconds to tell me who you are and what you're doing on my property before I shoot out your kneecaps and let the vultures finish you."

Ever so slowly, Kelly reached for her service weapon and made her way to the path. "You're surrounded, Seth. I want you face down on the ground with your hands behind your back. Make any sudden moves and I'll allow Mr. Oakes to make good on his vulture threat. Orson, call the sheriff and have him send out a few men to pick up Seth here and to collect JD from his house. Evan, can you call Conner and fill him in?"

As she expected, Seth didn't put up a fight, and within minutes he was bound, with Evan keeping a close eye on him. Kelly spoke to Jed. He'd explained noticing unfamiliar vehicle lights as he returned to his house from the barn, and decided to investigate.

"Kelly?" a soft voice asked from the direction of the caves.

"Kiara?" Kelly replied, afraid to hope and yet not able to keep herself from walking toward the voice that sounded like her sister.

"Kelly!" The voice grew stronger as Kelly moved closer and she gasped as her sister stepped out of the shadows.

"It is you! I thought I heard you and then I wasn't sure because I saw *him* outside of the cave."

Kelly threw her arms around her sister. "I was so scared. I thought I'd never see you again." She pulled back and ran her hands over the sides of Kiara's face. She looked fine. No bruises or anything. Holding on to her sister's shoulders, Kelly looked over the rest of her. "Are you okay? Nothing broken?"

"No, nothing like that." Kiara shook her head. "I never want to see another cave for as long as I live."

"I can't say I blame you. What happened?"

"I was stupid. I ran into Seth after lunch and he was talking about a horse he was watching and how she was ready to have a baby. Then he called when I got back to my room after the meetings were over and said she was in labor if I wanted to come. When I made it to the field, he was waiting and that other guy came from behind and grabbed me." She sniffled. "I was so scared, but I knew you'd come for me."

Kelly pulled her into a tight hug as flashing lights of the approaching first responders came into view. "Always."

Chapter Eighteen

Six Weeks Later

"ARE you sure you're okay with me being in Wilmington this weekend?" Kelly asked her sister.

"I'm fine," Kiara said. "You know mom and dad won't let anyone get to me. Especially since it looks like a security store gave birth in their house. Don't you think you went a wee bit overboard?"

"Just because they couldn't find a link between Randy and those two bozos from the ranch doesn't mean there isn't one."

It still turned Kelly's stomach to think about that first weekend at the ranch. JD had confessed to masterminding the kidnapping after overhearing a conversation about Kiara's past. He claimed he planned to call Randy the day after they took her and 'bargain' for her.

Since Randy claimed no knowledge and had that airtight alibi there was no reason to think otherwise. But that didn't mean Kelly agreed. Hence the increase in security at her parents's house. It was probably for the best her parents and Kiara didn't know about the undercover guard she also had watching the place.

"Whatever," Kiara said. "I know it's because you love me. Speaking of that four-letter 'L' word, will you be seeing your man this weekend?"

"Yes," she said on the ending of a blissful sigh.

Her man. It still blew her mind to think of Evan that way but there you had it. He was her man. Her long distance, sexy as hell, man.

After Kiara returned to the ranch, life became rather dull considering how their time had started out. Evan and Kiara both worked until the beginning of August when they had to return to their respective schools to prepare for the new school year. Kelly continued to stay over weekends until Kiara left.

She never thought she would miss Evan as bad as she did.

They had agreed to try the long distance thing but so far that consisted of endless texts messages and phone calls. This weekend would be the first time in over three weeks since they'd seen each other.

"Is everyone you know getting married or is that just an excuse to go back to Wilmington?" Kiara teased.

Kelly had to laugh. "No, this is the last one on my calendar." Someone knocked on her hotel door. "Evan's here. Bye." She hung up not even waiting to hear Kiara's goodbye.

She nearly tripped in her haste to make it to the door, but she got it open without breaking anything.

Damn, he'd grown even more handsome in three weeks. He looked entirely too delicious in his dark suit and tie.

"Wow," he said. "You look amazing."

She felt her cheeks heat. Only Evan could make her blush. "Thank you."

Cole and Sasha were having an outdoor wedding, so she'd opted to wear a sundress. It was light blue and the gauzy material made her feel like royalty. Plus, Kiara started to cry when Kelly came out of the dressing room to ask her opinion on how it looked. She took the tears as a good sign.

"You do too, handsome." She rose to her toes and gave him a quick kiss. Or at least, that was her intention. But Evan grabbed her low around the waist, letting out a sexy as fuck moan when his hand met nothing but skin, and her intentions flew straight out the window.

"I knew picking you up at your hotel was a bad idea," he said, pulling back for air. "How much time until the wedding starts?"

"Not long enough." Kelly stepped outside and closed the door.

"This is why you should have stayed with me at my house."

"The two of us under the same roof? Yeah, we'd *never* be late then." He'd asked her repeatedly to stay with him while she was in town and every time she'd turned him down. Though not for the reason he probably thought.

She didn't want to get used to being around him so much

again, knowing it would hurt like hell when she left. Now that he was in front of her, she realized her mistake.

It would hurt like hell, regardless.

Reluctantly, they made their way to his car.

COLE AND SASHA had planned a small, intimate wedding. Only Julie and Dena stood at the alter as bridesmaids and beside Cole were two men: Daniel and Jeff. Their vows were traditional, but everyone choked up when Cole recited his. Odds were, he didn't even realize the handful of tears running unashamed down his cheek.

Afterward, Kelly heard several people comment they never noticed how beautiful Sasha was before today. It was true; she had a glow about her that looked way beyond the normal one shared by brides. The thing was, Cole had the same glow, it was just harder to pick out because the woman at his side naturally drew your eyes.

"It's love." Dena held her youngest daughter while watching Jeff twirl around the dance floor with their oldest, both father and child laughing as they spun.

"She's more than beautiful," Kelly said, watching as the bride shared a kiss with her new husband. "She's radiant."

"She's not the only one," Evan whispered in her ear. Kelly lifted her head to smile at him and he dropped his head to steal a kiss.

"That's a sight I never thought I'd see," someone said from behind them and they turned to find a grinning Daniel and Julie. "I all but called Orson a liar when he told me about you two. 'Are we talking about the same Kelly and Evan?' I asked him. 'Short spitfire with red hair?' He almost had me convinced until he started talking about some demo you two supposedly did. Then I knew he was talking about a different couple. Ow," he said to his wife. "Why did you pinch me?"

Julie smiled but remained silent.

"Anyway," Daniel said. "It's always good to see you, Kelly. Don't be a stranger."

"I wouldn't dream of it," she replied and she swore Daniel winked at Evan.

It was probably her imagination, but even so she waited until Daniel and Julie were speaking to someone else before asking Evan, "Did Daniel *wink* at you?"

"Nah," he said. "I'm sure he didn't. Probably something in his eye."

She glanced over to where Daniel stood talking with several people, his arm casually draped around Julie. Maybe, but his eye looked fine.

"Come here," Evan said, pulling her close to him and whispering, "Would it be rude if we left right now?"

"We should probably stay for dinner." Not that she didn't want to leave with Evan, but it was a small wedding so they'd be missed, plus, she wasn't sure when she'd be back in Wilmington and she wanted to spend a little more time with her friends.

There was a difference being back in Wilmington this time as opposed to when she was for Daniel and Julie's wedding. Then she was still unsettled with her move. Whereas now she enjoyed her job and the people she worked with. She loved being so close to her parents and her sister. To be honest, she was still living with Kiara because there was no reason to run out and buy a new place and the two of them got along great.

The only thing wrong with Dallas was that Evan wasn't there.

Dinner was a sit down meal, but there were no place cards. Kelly overheard Sasha telling someone, "I think everyone's smart enough to find a place to sit without being told how to do it. As long as I'm next to Cole, I don't care where anyone sits."

Kelly and Evan found seats at a table with Nathaniel and Abby West and their two children, Elizabeth and Henry. The couple welcomed them warmly and Kelly was glad they had the opportunity to sit with them. Since leaving town, she hadn't had the chance to catch up with Abby.

"I can't believe how much Elizabeth and Henry have grown since I last saw them," Kelly said. "Looking at them, you'd think I've been gone years instead of months."

Abby laughed. "They're like weeds. I don't see it since I'm with them every day, but I can tell because they keep outgrowing their clothes so fast."

Henry leaned over to Elizabeth and said in a loud whisper, "Mama called us weeds."

Elizabeth rolled her eyes and said back, "She said we're *like* weeds. It's a figure of speech called a simile. You grow fast and weeds grow fast."

Henry nodded and repeated, "simile," several times.

"And too precocious for their own good," Abby added and

leaned over so they couldn't hear. "It's getting to be quite a feat to find quality time with Nathaniel."

"I don't doubt it," Kelly said back in her own whisper.

"Mama, you said whispers weren't nice," Henry said.

"You're right," Abby said and then mumbled under her breath, "Next time we'll just go to the ladies' room and chat there."

They didn't have to end up making a break for the ladies' room. Nathaniel got both Henry and Elizabeth talking by asking them where they wanted to go for a long weekend before school started.

"Disney World!" Henry shouted.

"Alaska," Elizabeth said at the same time.

While Nathaniel and Evan discussed pros and cons of both places with the two children, Abby leaned close and asked Kelly, "Are things working out with you and Evan?"

Kelly sighed. "Too soon to tell. I really want it to, but this long distance stuff is hard."

"How does he feel?"

"We haven't really talked about it." They needed to, she knew. Unfortunately, when she finally got Evan alone, she didn't want to talk. "But we have to make time."

Abby gave her hand a squeeze. "It'll all work out like it's supposed to. I've found life is sneaky like that."

Kelly hoped that would be the case.

THEY LEFT SHORTLY after dinner ended. Kelly told

everyone goodbye and gave hugs. She couldn't help but think a few of her old friends looked as if they knew something but weren't telling her.

"Is there something going on with the group?" she asked Evan once they were in his car and headed back to his place. They'd already agreed before the wedding to stop at his house for a bit before going back to her hotel.

"What do you mean?" Evan asked.

"I'm not sure, I just got the feeling there was an inside joke or something I wasn't aware of."

"I haven't heard of any jokes."

Now that she'd brought it up and they were talking about it, Evan seemed a bit off, too. "Maybe not a joke," she added. "But something's going on." She didn't tell him she thought he was also in on whatever it was.

Though she had a feeling she should have told him before now how very much she detested surprises.

Evan lived in a townhouse. She'd been to it before as they had held several group meetings at his place in years past. He'd never hosted a party, however.

He parked in front of the well-kept brick building and Kelly searched her mind for something normal to say. Something that didn't refer to the past when they were always bickering and didn't highlight her growing suspicion that he was keeping something from her. And that most certainly didn't talk about an unknown and undiscussed future.

"Are you ready for the new school year?" She finally decided on as he unlocked his front door, thinking jobs were relatively safe. "Do you have a list of the students you'll be teaching?"

He didn't answer but pushed the door open. Kelly stepped inside and froze. His townhouse was almost empty and there were packed boxes everywhere.

"No," he said. "I'm actually not teaching this year."

It took her brain a second to catch up. "You're moving."

She made herself stare at the boxes because if she didn't she'd look at him and he'd know. He'd know exactly how much it hurt that he was moving and hadn't brought it up to her even once.

"I didn't want to tell you before the wedding," Evan said.

She nodded, still looking at the boxes. Yeah, sure. That made sense. What made little sense was something else he said. "You said you're not teaching this year. You're moving and you don't have a job lined up?" Who did that?

"I said I wasn't teaching this year. I never said I didn't have a job." He moved a half-filled box from the couch to the floor. "Come over here and sit down."

What was his problem? Why did he sound so happy? She risked a peek at him. No, it was something beyond happy. He was excited. She plopped down on the couch, not understanding anything that had happened in the last few minutes.

"I had a call from Orson last weekend," Evan said. "He's always had plans to open places like the ranch. He asked me after graduation to go in with him on his Vegas venture. I didn't. I had too many student loans, that sort of thing. When he called last weekend, he indicated he was still looking for a business partner and wanted to know if I was interested."

She remembered him saying they had been college roommates, but didn't recall anything about a business proposition.

"I'm much better off financially now," Evan said. "My loans have been repaid and I've made some good investments. I live simply. So I told him yes. The way I see it, why not? I'm young and don't have any kids. Besides, the woman I love is there."

"Where?"

"In Texas," he said. "It's not Dallas, but it's a hell of a lot closer than Wilmington."

"You're moving to Texas." The words tasted foreign on her tongue but with time, she would get used to them. She repeated his words in her head, and then out loud. "You're moving to Texas and you love me."

"I do, Kelly, and the long distance thing is killing me. I probably should have told you but I thought it'd be a nice surprise."

A nice surprise.

Before Evan, she'd have augured that there was no such thing. And though she claimed to hate surprises, being with Evan meant a new surprise almost every day. Maybe they weren't as bad as she thought.

She moved into his lap and straddled him. "It's more than a nice surprise. It's the best ever surprise. And here's another one: I love you, too."

"That's no surprise, K," he said, his eyes teasing her. "I

knew from the moment you first called me dickwad it was only a matter of time."

She punched his shoulder. "You did not."

"Okay, maybe not the *first* time."

"You are so full of it."

"Spank me."

She pulled back to study his expression. "You know better."

"Maybe I do. Maybe I don't."

"Then I must see to it you do in the future."

She lowered her head to kiss him and saw snippets of their future flash behind her closed eyes. They would never be like their friends. Neither of them would ever wear the other's collar. Any use of 'Master' or 'Mistress' would be limited to whatever scene they were in.

No one would know what to call them and that was fine.

The best things she was learning, were undefinable.

Epilogue

Evan hoped Kelly wasn't going to ask him again if he was sure he wanted to do this because if she did, he'd end up spanking her, and that was not how this afternoon was supposed to go. At the moment, he was on his knees in the living room of the cottage he'd stayed in over the summer. He'd moved back into it following his move to Texas a month ago.

At the time his plan had been to look for a permanent place to live, but that had been before Orson offered Kelly a job as the head of his security team. She hadn't decided one way or the other. Until she did, he'd put his house hunting on hold. The hope being if she said yes, that they would move in together.

The sound of heels clicking against hardwoods drove all thoughts but one from his mind.

Fucking hell, she had her boots on.

Ordinarily, he'd drink in the sight of her for as long as he wanted, but he couldn't at present. Fortunately, she walked close enough to where he knelt that he could see the leather toes. He bit back a moan. *She probably had her leather corset on, too.*

"Well now," Kelly said, and the tip of what he assumed was a riding crop traced the line of his spine. "It looks like someone is happy."

He was naked. If he wanted to lie about how hard he was at the moment, it would be impossible. But she hadn't asked him a question, so he stayed still and silent.

"And it appears as if someone is trying to be very good." The crop went back up his spine. "Too bad you've already earned a spanking. Although, if you behave and continue to be good, I might do something about that hard dick. Would you like that?"

"Yes, Ma'am," he said, his heart beating like mad.

Just as he would never be her Master, she would never be his Mistress. They had agreed to use "Sir" and "Ma'am" at times such as this.

"Very nice," she said. "Stand and bend over, placing your hands on your knees or thighs. Whichever is more comfortable. However, you do not have permission to look at me. Understand?"

What? He had to stop from saying. Why couldn't he look at her?

"Yes, Ma'am," he said anyway. He understood what she wanted him to do, or, in this case, what she didn't want him to do, he just didn't understand why.

But as he rose to his feet, it hit him that at this particular time it wasn't his place to understand. All she required of him was obedience.

It was a freeing revelation.

He had never placed a sub in the position Kelly asked him to take. Once he was in place with his feet shoulder width apart and hands on his knees, he wondered why that was. He didn't have to see himself to know what an awesome position it was for the Top. As for the bottom? Being bent over the way he was, he knew exactly how vulnerable it felt.

"I like you this way." Kelly was all around him as she spoke. Her hands ran across his back even as her words washed over him. "All quiet and compliant."

She reached his ass and raked her nails across his backside. She kept her nails short and trimmed but somehow he still felt them. And damn they felt good. He closed his eyes, but that didn't stop his awareness of how much harder he grew.

An awareness Kelly shared. "Looks like I'm not the only one who likes it."

The first slap of her hand on his ass caught him off guard with the strength behind it, and he almost broke position. Fortunately, he caught himself in time. The second one he was prepared for. By the fifth one, he wanted to have a nice face-to-face with the Evan that told her she hit like a girl. No, he would tell that Evan, she hit like a woman, and women hit just like men, the difference was, you weren't expecting it, and that's why it felt harder. By the tenth one, he decided, no, that wasn't it. Women hit harder. And by the time he'd counted fifteen, he didn't care one way or the other because instead of number sixteen, she went back to using her nails and all he could concentrate on was not coming on himself.

"I didn't know it was possible for you to get any harder." Kelly gave his cock a squeeze, and he almost bit his tongue off in an attempt not to spew all over her hand. "I was wrong."

He wondered if that was all she had planned. Part of him hoped it was because her touch on him was so fucking good, he'd promise her anything to feel it again. But part of him hoped it wasn't because he was on a high like he'd never experienced.

She moved to stand behind him. "Lift your head and stare at the smoke detector on the ceiling."

She wasn't done. He lifted his head and found the smoke detector. When she slapped the crop against his upper thighs, he bit back a moan.

"You didn't think I was finished with you, did you?" she teased.

This time, even though she used a crop, she went lighter on him than she did with her hands. In many ways it was worse because after every few strikes of the crop, she'd use her hands and sensually tease his flesh.

He was the only passenger on a runaway train and he was getting ready to run out of track.

"Please, Ma'am," he begged. "I need to come."

"No." She ran a finger from behind his cock to his ass. *Ah fuck.* "Quiet," she said even though he didn't remember saying anything out loud. "Maybe one day I'll fuck your ass. You'd like that wouldn't you?"

Before today the answer would have been a resounding no. Now he wasn't so sure he'd hate it and part of him was already certain he'd love it.

"I think you've been pretty good, so I've decided to let you come. Do you want my mouth or my hand?"

"Your mouth, Ma'am."

He felt her walk around him. She hadn't told him to stop looking at the smoke detector so he wasn't able to watch her walk, but he pictured it in his head.

"Look at me," she finally said.

He dropped his head, and nearly came on the spot.

He'd been right about the boots, but wrong about everything else. She wasn't wearing a corset. She wasn't wearing anything other than the boots.

"Holy fuck you're gorgeous, Ma'am. I almost feel as if looking at you is rewarding enough."

She gave a soft laugh. "I don't have to blow you if you'd rather I not."

"No way," he said. "I believe my words were *almost enough.*"

"So you did," she said, sinking to her knees before him and not giving him a chance to catch his breath before taking him into her mouth.

· · ·

LATER THAT NIGHT as they sat outside on his private patio watching the stars come out, she turned to him. "I've decided I'm going to accept Orson's offer."

His heart sang and he felt like she had lifted a weight off him. "I'm so glad," he told her. "That was what I was hoping you would do."

"You know this means we'll have to find a place to live we can both agree on."

He raised an eyebrow. "Do you think that'll be hard?"

"You have met us, haven't you?" She laughed.

"I don't think it'll be that hard. After all, look at what we've already been through."

"I want a pink bathroom."

"Oh hell, no. Not a pink bathroom." Was she serious?

"See what I mean? We don't agree on anything."

He reached for her hand and pulled her into his lap. "You're wrong," he said. "We're completely in agreement on what counts. I can't explain it with words though, I'll have to show you. And it'll take some time. I'm thinking the next forever or two."

She ran her fingers into his hair. "Lucky for you, I happen to be free for the next forever or two."

"Lucky for *us*," he whispered before sealing their words with a kiss.

Kɪᴀʀᴀ ᴀɴᴅ Oʀsᴏɴ will return late 2019! Don't miss it, sign up for my newsletter here.

Acknowledgments

I didn't want to write this book.

I'm not sure why. I'd always had a lot of fun writing Evan and Kelly in the past. Maybe it was because they were both Tops and I wasn't sure how that was going to work out. Maybe it was because I feared they wouldn't be any fun once they stopped fighting. Maybe it was because it was getting to be such a long time since the last Submissive Series novel, I thought people would either have forgotten it ("Submissive, who?") or that they'd roll their eyes ("Another one? You've got to be kidding me.")

But, you. Yes, you, the readers of the series, would not let go of Evan and Kelly. You were determined that they get their happily-ever-after and you weren't afraid to let me know. Eventually, I decided to stop fighting and instead to get busy writing. After all, you are my audience, and if people have forgotten about the series, maybe this would be a pleasant reminder. And to those who roll their eyes?

Well, I'm made of tougher stuff.

Besides, I'm finding in my old age it's a lot more fun to do whatever the hell I want and ignore those that think I can be stopped with an eye roll.

So there I was, writing a book I didn't really want to but determined to make myself do it, when the craziest thing happened.

I began to like it. It became fun. And then the most craziest thing happened.

I fell in love with Evan and Kelly.

Trust me, no one was more surprised than me.

Those that know me know I don't do much of an outline, but as I've matured as a writer, I always feel like it's one of those things I should do. I attempted to 'outline' once again while writing this and, as always, it changed every other day. I've learned to just go with it. I always assume it's the characters telling me how things really happened and they've never steered me wrong.

I hope you enjoyed reading Evan and Kelly's story. It was a joy to write and I'm certain it's not the last we've heard from these two.

Finally, as an author who has written and continues to write primarily BDSM fiction, one of the first questions I'm always asked is whether I'm in the lifestyle or if I have been in the past. The answer to both questions is no. However, I've had many excellent teachers. Because of confidentiality, I won't name you here, but you know who you are. I thank you for the gift of your advice and experiences.

Tara

WALL STREET ROYALS

"…so damn HOT and intense, what an amazing start to a series…"
The Sassy Nerd Review on FOK

Wall Street Royals

FOK
Book One

Big Swinging D
Book Two

Conquer. Control. Command. They have. They are. They will. They are the Wall Street Royals, men at the top of their game who are about to be mastered by the one thing they never counted on: love.

Don't miss this seductively sexy new series by New York Times bestselling author Tara Sue Me.

AMERICAN ASSHOLE

"Scorching sex, well-developed characters, occasional bursts of humor, and skillful plotting make Me's series launch a must-read." - PUBLISHERS WEEKLY

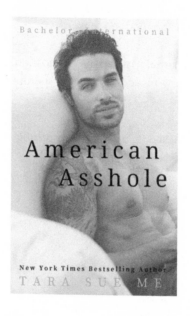

He groaned my name as he pressed deeper inside me and I fisted the white sheets so tightly my knuckles almost matched their color.

We shouldn't be doing this, but more importantly *I* shouldn't be doing this. I should have never let it get this far. I knew better.

I should have never said yes to dinner. I should have never

said yes to this trip. I should have never said yes to the contract.

But damn it all I had, even knowing what it would cost us both.

His weight pressed me into the mattress and his breath was hot in my ear. "Are you still with me?" Then for good measure he shifted his hips so his next thrust hit a new spot inside me and I moaned in pleasure.

It seemed I was unable to say no to the man. Nor did I want to. My body moved with his, desperate to draw him deeper.

"Are you?" he asked again, his lips brushing my nape and sending shivers down my spine.

"Yes. Oh, God, yes."

ALSO BY TARA SUE ME

THE SUBMISSIVE SERIES:

The Submissive

The Dominant

The Training

The Chalet*

Seduced by Fire

The Enticement

The Collar

The Exhibitionist

The Master

The Exposure

The Claiming*

The Flirtation

Mentor's Match

The Mentor & The Master*

Top Trouble

RACK ACADEMY SERIES:

Master Professor

Headmaster

BACHELOR INTERNATIONAL:

American Asshole

THE DATE DUO:

The Date Dare

The Date Deal

WALL STREET ROYALS:

FOK

Big Swinging D

OTHERS:

Her Last Hello

Altered Allies (currently unavailable)

Writing as Tara Thomas

Shattered Fear*

Hidden Fate*

Twisted End*

Darkest Night

Deadly Secret

Broken Promise

*eNovella

ABOUT THE AUTHOR

NEW YORK TIMES/USA TODAY BESTSELLING AUTHOR

Even though she graduated with a degree in science, Tara knew she'd never be happy doing anything other than writing. Specifically, writing love stories.

She started with a racy BDSM story and found she was not quite prepared for the unforeseen impact it would have. Nonetheless, she continued and The Submissive Series novels would go on to be both *New York Times* and *USA Today* Bestsellers. One of those, THE MASTER, was a 2017 RITA finalist for Best Erotic Romance. Well over one million copies of her books have been sold worldwide.

www.tarasueme.com

Made in the USA
Las Vegas, NV
18 February 2021

18083077R00121